LOVE ON A TRAIN

WAGON WHEEL JUSTICE

BLYTHE CARVER

1

———

Taylor Jameson stretched his long legs as he picked through the mail. He and his mother, Julia, had relocated to Sacramento just one year ago and were enjoying the change of weather from New York, where it was often damp, rainy, and cold. He stood on the front stoop of his large home, fingering through the few envelopes.

He halted on one envelope and yanked it from the rest, hurrying through the doorway and into his home. He crossed the foyer, glancing toward the doors of the dining room on his left and the parlor to his right.

"Mother?" he called out. "Are you in here?"

He heard nothing from either room and

continued on toward his study. As he passed the stairs to the second floor, he called up the stairs. "Mother. You there?"

"What is it?" he heard the faint voice of his mother coming from a room up there, likely the playroom, where his two children would be playing.

"Come to the study, please."

Taylor didn't have to tell Julia why he needed her to come down. She would already know. The letter he held in his hand would make the third in as many months.

The enemy had found them.

Two years ago, Taylor's wife, Becky, was murdered on a train bound for Oklahoma, where she was going to visit a friend. Shortly after, letters began to arrive, demanding something unknown to Taylor. It was unclear if the letters were associated with the murder or not because no link was ever found between them. This happened while Taylor lived with his family in New York.

Feeling the danger had become too great, Taylor took his children, Bella, aged five, and Alex, aged four, along with his mother, Julia, across the country to Sacramento, where an uncle had started a successful law firm. It was impossible to run his import/export business in New York when he was across the country in California, so he'd entrusted the business to an associate until the situation with the threatening letters was resolved.

He stood by the window in his office, looking down at the letter for a few moments before sliding a sharp letter opener under the flap of the envelope and ripping it open. He slid the letter out and set the envelope, which was addressed the same as all the others, with only his name and address on the front, along with the stamp and postmark, on the desk behind him.

His mother hurried into the room, closing the door softly behind her.

"What does it say?" she asked without hesitation.

Taylor read from the letter.

"You cannot avoid us by running away. We will have what we want. We are becoming impatient. Contact us through paper. Ignore this at your own peril. It says nothing else." He tossed the paper on the desk, and his mother swept it up into her hands, glaring at it with hatred.

"They aren't going to leave us alone. We have to find out who is sending them and what they want. Have you heard anything from the men investigating the murder?"

"They haven't found a link between the letters

and Becky, if that's what you're asking," Taylor said, irritation sliding through him. That always happened when he thought about the lawmen looking into his wife's death. She hadn't been carrying anything of value that he knew of, no documents or large amounts of cash. No jewelry was taken that anyone was aware of. She'd been found strangled in a compartment on the train with no sign of a killer anywhere. At least not by the time police got on the train.

"You need to call Wagon Wheel Justice," Julia stated, tossing the letter down with the same disdain her son had used. "They will find out who is behind this."

Taylor screwed up his face, moving his eyes from the busy street outside his window to her face. "What are you talking about, Mother?"

"Wagon Wheel Justice Agency. It was an investigative service run by Gabriel Salinger, a good friend of your uncle's. He left the agency to his nieces, and they are supposed to be very good at what they do. I think it's worth your while, son. No matter the cost."

Taylor snorted softly. "No matter the cost does not sound good, Mother. How much is this going to take from me?"

"You have enough," Julia continued. "Your business still thrives, and we eat well. Money is not the problem. We both know that. You won't object to working with women, will you, Taylor?"

Taylor gazed at his mother. He knew her facial expressions well, and when she narrowed her eyes at him, he knew he better respond the right way or suffer her wrath. "I have no issue working with a woman, and you know that. If they are smart women, I have no issue, that is. There's nothing I cannot tolerate more than a brainless woman."

"The same goes for a man, I say," Julia added.

He nodded. "Yes, that, too. Insufferable fools in business who don't know one thing about how to turn a profit." He shook his head, recalling a few anecdotes in his mind of experiences with just such fools in his past.

"I will go by in the morning," he said, "and request a meeting. Would you like to be present for it?"

"You know I would," Julia replied, "but if I am needed for the children, I really must do what is required of me. They are my charges now that Becky was taken from them."

Taylor's heart seized briefly at his mother's last sentence. His children resembled his now deceased wife in minor but significant ways, like Bella's eyebrows were shaped the same, and Alex had Becky's smile. It was those subtle things that made him more determined to keep her alive to their children.

2

Josie Salinger looked around the kitchen, scanning the plates of her sisters to see if any of them needed any more eggs, bacon, or biscuits. She enjoyed getting up in the mornings and making breakfast for them and for herself. Now they had Larson, her sister Sadie's fiancé, and Cody, Adelaide's fiancé, who was only there for breakfast on occasion. Larson was the bodyguard for the sisters and their detective agency as a whole, so he stayed in the large house with them. The back of the three-story building served as a home for the sisters, while the front was the office space for the agency. They were connected by a narrow corridor between the two halves of the building.

"Any of you want more?" she asked.

"I'll take two more biscuits if you have them," Larson answered with a smile, lifting one long arm in the air.

"Biscuit hog," Sadie hissed, leaning forward and grinning at her beau. He grinned back.

"I can't help it. She knows how to cook biscuits, this one."

"Thank you," Josie sang the words. She returned to the table with two biscuits on her plate, which she transferred to his before she sat down. "I've been waiting for you all to try my gravy recipe. What do you think?"

"It's mighty tasty," Larson exclaimed. Sadie froze and stared at him with wide eyes. The rest of the women followed suit, letting the man know he's said something wrong. They were only teasing him, but their silent staring treatment worked as planned when he also stopped what he was doing and swept his eyes around the table. "What?" he asked. "What did I say?"

"Well, you are full of compliments for my sister this morning, aren't you?" Sadie asked.

Josie just grinned, relaxing her face and resting her eyes. "Oh, he doesn't mean anything. He's only being nice."

"Of course I'm being nice. I'm always nice." He picked up one of the biscuits she'd set down for him and used it to jab the air at Josie. "You are a good cook. Your sisters *should* be jealous."

"All right, children. Enough of that."

Adelaide came through the doorway at that moment, a towel in her hands. Josie assumed she'd been washing up.

"Are you very hungry this morning?" she asked. "I made you a plate. It's covered over there."

"That was sweet of you, sister," Adelaide replied, flashing a big grin her way. "I am very hungry, as a matter of fact. And I'm wondering if we're going to have anything exciting happening this week. It's been so calm for the last few weeks, no work. Makes me feel dull being idle. I want to get my hands into something."

"I know what you mean," Belinda, the quiet one of the four sisters, spoke up. "I've been volunteering my time so that I don't get bored. I feel terrible, though, wishing we had work. That usually means something is wrong in someone's life, and we're obliged to investigate it. So good news for us means someone has gotten some bad news."

"That's a unique way to look at it," Larson said,

holding the biscuit to his lips and speaking before devouring the bit he had left.

"It's true, though," Adelaide said, sliding into her seat with her plate in hand.

"I've been thinking about volunteering, too," Josie said. "If something doesn't come—"

Between the office section of the house and the residence section, a bell had been stretched so that when someone was at the front door, it would ring in the back of the house. The loud sound rang through the dining area, making Belinda jump.

She giggled. "I'll never get used to that sound," she murmured.

Josie continued to eat but stopped cold when her sisters looked at her.

"Is it... my turn?" she asked, feeling her stomach churn. She knew the day would come. She'd been dreading it since they took the company over just ten short months ago. Her sisters, Sadie and Adelaide, were both older than her and very much the take charge sisters. Adelaide was exceedingly sharp, as was Sadie, and each had their own methods of investigation that had proven successful in the cases they'd had so far.

Josie was expected to do more than look nice and serve coffee when clients came by. She had to take part in an investigation, despite her withdrawn, shy nature.

"I... I don't want to..." she murmured, hoping her sisters would take pity on her if she sounded child-like enough. "Please don't make me." The thought of meeting a stranger at the door and assessing their need made her feel a little sick. She suddenly wished she hadn't eaten half her breakfast already. "It's so early," she protested weakly. "Too early for all that thinking."

"It's time, Josie," Adelaide, who was the oldest, said in an "I'm the oldest sister" voice she sometimes used when she wanted one of them to do something and wouldn't take no for an answer.

"But..." It was futile, and she knew it. The sharp looks she was getting from Adelaide and Sadie were packed with meaning. She knew they were only doing what was best for her. "All right, all right," she said, pushing her chair back.

At least Larson was giving her a sympathetic look. She kept that look in mind as she went through the door and started down the corridor to the front of the building.

She emerged from the corridor at the same time as the client outside rang the bell again. It made her jump this time, and she drew in a quick breath. She stopped in the small foyer. Two double doors led to a second foyer, then another set of double doors opened to the outside.

Josie closed her eyes and willed her heart to stop pounding so hard. It was just a client interested in their services. It wasn't like a monster was going to grab her and eat her up.

Even if it felt like that.

She let out her breath slowly, relaxing her shoulders and rolling her head from side to side, trying to loosen up.

"I can do this," she mumbled, pulling open both double doors and marching through as if she was full of confidence. She pretended her heart wasn't about to come out of her chest as she pulled the right side door open and smiled at the man standing on the other side.

At first, she was speechless. She was taken aback by how attractive he was. He was tall, slender, dressed in a fine suit with a top hat and a fancy overcoat. A November breeze smacked her in the face, and she knew why he was wearing the overcoat.

"P-please come in," she said, "get out of the cold. I'm sorry to make you wait out here." She scanned him as he smiled and passed her by, taking off his hat as he entered. His wavy brown hair was fairly long, reaching down past his collar to his shoulders. She noticed the flash of his brown eyes when he turned once he was beyond the second set of double doors.

"Thank you. I'm sorry to come so early. I hope I haven't interrupted anything."

Josie shook her head, closing the doors securely. "Not at all. I was unaware of how cool it had gotten. I'm relatively new to Sacramento, having only been here a year or so."

"Really?" The man tilted his head to the side, looking interested. "I have also only been here a year." He stepped forward. "Taylor Jameson. I'd like to employ your company to do some investigating for me."

Josie smiled at him, shaking his hand. It was easier than she'd thought it would be. "Josie Salinger. Come into the office here and tell me what's going on."

3

Taylor examined the offices subtly as he walked through the foyer and into the largest one behind Josie Salinger. She was a nice looking woman, notably with violet eyes, which he rarely saw, and dark hair that was currently swaying behind her, pulled back in a large barrette. Dressed simply and comfortably in a green and blue frock with black slippers on her feet, he thought she was quite attractive.

The thoughts of her appearance were fleeting, however, as Taylor's worries about his family and the threatening letters were first and foremost in his mind.

He sat down in the chair opposite the large desk and was a little surprised when the woman sat in the other chair instead of going around the desk and sitting in the big chair. She leaned to the side and smiled at him.

"Please tell me what your need is."

"I'm receiving threatening letters," he said, admiring the fact that she was a down-to-business kind of lady. He reached in his breast pocket and pulled three envelopes from there, producing them for her. She took them and sat back in the chair, going through them one by one as he talked. "I've been getting these for the past few months here in Sacramento. I moved my family from New York a year ago to escape these letters, but somehow they've found me again. I don't know what they want, and I really don't know what they mean by contacting them through the paper."

"Has it gone any further than the letters?" Josie asked, glancing up at him. "Has there been any actual... threat carried out against you or your family?"

Taylor shifted in his seat, thinking of Becky. He'd practiced all the way there that morning, trying to figure out the best way to explain what was going on without sounding like a confused lunatic.

"My wife Becky was murdered on a train two years ago," he said. "The letters didn't come until after. They started about three months after she was... killed." He swallowed, determined not to let his emotions get the better of him. "We've been searching for a connection to her murder with the letters but so far haven't found one. The detectives and lawmen investigating the murder haven't found a link, but I'm not really sure they are looking that hard. That's why I'm here. I need someone focused on these letters and finding out where they are coming from and what these men want."

"You don't know if it's connected to your wife's murder?"

"No." Taylor shook his head, feeling remorseful. "I wish I did. If there was any way I could have saved Becky, I would have. I loved her."

"I'm sure you did," Josie replied in a kind voice that made him feel a bit better. He struggled to bring his thoughts back into focus.

"I think it has something to do with her murder. I searched her study after she was gone, but I didn't find anything that might make me think she was getting letters like these before she died. I thought maybe if someone was trying to blackmail her or extort money or jewelry from her, I might find a letter stating that. But if she got anything like that, she burned it. I found nothing."

Josie stood up and went around the desk. He watched her shuffle through a desk drawer and pull out a notepad and a pen. She set the pad on the desk and wrote down his name, his wife's name, and a few words underneath. She pointed at the letters with the pen, looking at him.

"Are these the only letters you have received?"

Taylor nodded. "The only ones from here in Sacramento. I have quite a few from New York."

"And when did you start receiving them?"

"My wife died in January," Taylor responded, ignoring the pain that recalling everything was creating in his heart. This had to be done. He had to pursue another line of investigation since the lawmen assigned to the case were getting nowhere after two years. He could only hope there was still time to find out who was responsible. Two years was a long time to go without finding any evidence. "We started getting the letters three months later."

Josie looked up at him from her notepad. "We?"

"I live with my two children and my mother. I said we because my mother has always been a big part of my life and is the one who recommended I come to your agency in the first place. Her brother knew your father and said he was a good man. Mother says you are his nieces and are also respectable and smart. We need some help on our side. Someone who will focus on this one crime. The lawmen have too many other crimes to deal with. We need focus and concentration."

"Do you think finding the person responsible for writing the letters will lead us to your wife's killer or killers?" Josie asked.

"Yes, that's what I believe."

Josie nodded. "All right. Let me write this down. The letters were started a few months after your wife died, so about March or April?"

"Yes, that's right."

"Of this year or last year?"

"Last year."

"All right. And you moved here to Sacramento when?"

"About a year ago, December of last year."

Josie wrote the dates down. "And these letters started arriving three months ago."

"Yes, that's right."

Josie sat for a moment. Taylor could tell she was thinking. He scanned her face, wondering if her sisters looked like her. His mother had said there were four of them, and each one had earned a good reputation in the months they had been running the agency. He was willing to trust her judgment and, so far, was impressed by the way this woman controlled herself. She wasn't flamboyant and outrageous in any way. He felt comfortable with her, and that was saying something for him. He was normally very reserved and shy. Since the death of his wife, he had become fiercely protective of his loved ones, keeping away from anything and anyone he deemed harmful to them in any way, emotionally, physically, spiritually. It didn't matter.

"I should probably get my sisters," she mumbled, her eyes on the notepad, the tip of the pen between her lips. She tapped it several times and then looked up at him. He wondered for a moment if she knew she'd spoken aloud. "I'm sure we would be happy to take this case on, Mr. Jameson. Do you know of our charges?"

"Money doesn't matter," Taylor replied, taking a blank check he'd already prepared out of his pocket, unfolding it, and laying it on the desk between them. He smoothed it out with both hands to remove the crease in the middle. "You put your fee on that line and take it to the bank. I have a successful company out of New York, and money is not a problem for me. I just want my family safe."

"I understand," Josie said, taking the check and sliding it into the middle drawer of the desk. "I do hope you understand that we will have to be asking some possibly personal questions. If you feel uncomfortable answering, just tell us, and we'll find another way to get our answers."

"I want to be completely open with you," Taylor responded. The longer he spent with Josie Salinger, the more he liked her take-charge attitude. She seemed to have a good head on her shoulders. He even liked her smooth handwriting, which he could see upside down on the notepad in front of her. "I appreciate you taking this on. I know the letter sounds quite tame, but I really do believe these are the same men who killed my wife. I know they will come after another member of my family."

"But what is it they want in exchange for leaving you alone?" Josie asked, picking up the letters, which she'd left unfolded on the desktop, and scanning through them.

"That's the thing," Taylor answered, knowing he sounded desperate. "I don't know. I can't figure it out."

"They've never mentioned it? Specifically what it is they want?"

Taylor shook his head. "No. Not once."

4

Josie was intrigued by the mystery surrounding the letters. She tried to reconcile the timeline in her mind. They'd escaped the letters after half a year of threats only for the threats to resume all the way across the country after seven or eight months of silence. Somehow they had found the Jameson family three thousand miles away from their home.

"I'm sure you keep in contact with people in New York, don't you?" Josie asked, folding the letters and sliding them back in their appropriate envelopes.

Taylor nodded. "I do. But I have limited contact with anyone there besides my business partner. He wouldn't reveal my address to anyone. I'm sure of it. A hundred percent sure of it."

"The first mystery we need to solve is how you were found."

"The first step in a long mystery, you mean," Taylor put in. He looked despondent.

Josie wished there was something she could say to comfort him, but she was on the verge of feeling overwhelmed. It wasn't like she'd ever taken the lead in a case before.

Taylor was a formidable character. He spoke with as much class as he dressed. If Josie wasn't so concerned about the predicament he was in, she would have been intimidated.

Instead of letting it get the better of her though, she was determined to show her sisters she had what it took to get the job done. Even if it was scaring her to death. She hoped she looked more confident than she felt.

She fiddled with the corner of the notepad, trying to think of where to start. Picking up the letters, she examined the postmarks.

"These letters are postmarked in New York," she said. "They were posted in New York. You say your wife was killed on a train coming from New York to Oklahoma or from Oklahoma to New York?"

"To Oklahoma," Taylor replied.

"Hmm," Josie pondered, tapping her chin with one finger.

"You don't think we'll have to go back to New York to figure this out, do you?"

"I don't know," Josie answered. "We might have to. Would you object to that?"

"I don't want to go back if my children aren't safe."

"There is no reason why you should have to take them back with you," Josie suggested. "You can leave them here with your mother, can't you?"

Taylor shook his head, a serious look on his long slender face. "No. I can't leave them. I'd be too far away from them if something were to happen. I would never forgive myself if these men came after my family while I was traveling back to New York. I can't leave them behind."

Josie understood what he was saying, even though she had no children or husband of her own. "I wouldn't want to leave my children either," she said. "I'll get my sisters, and we'll work out a plan."

"I want to be as involved with this as I can be," Taylor said, "I'm just not sure what I can do."

"The letters all say to get in touch with them through the paper," Josie remarked, thoughtfully. "I think we'll have to put an ad or a comment in the paper to let them know we've seen it. And that we're willing to work with them."

"But how are we going to do that? And how do I know they won't just shoot me on sight if they see me?"

"Clearly, they have already seen you," Josie responded. "I'm sure they had someone check your address physically and put their eyes on you to let the bad men know it's really you. And you shouldn't set up a meeting with them. You should have a liaison. A go-between. A middle-man. Only it will be a woman because I can meet with them for you."

"I don't think that's a good idea."

That was exactly what Josie expected him to say. And the fact that she'd even offered had surprised herself more than anything.

Taylor made her want to take initiative. He seemed to hold her in such high regard even after such a short period of time. He looked at her when he spoke to her, in the eye, without moving away uncomfortably. She could tell he wasn't dumbing down his words so that she would understand.

"I know you don't, and my sisters will probably object, too. But I'll be honest with you, Mr. Jameson—"

"Taylor," he interjected.

Josie halted and continued from there, "Taylor, let me be honest with you. If I take this case, it will be the first one I've been the primary on. My sisters say I don't do enough to participate in the company, and they want me to broaden my horizons. They also say that I'm too shy."

Taylor looked surprised by that.

"Yes, I am shy," she stated with a hint of mirth in her voice. "I think it would prove something to them if I put myself out there and got in a little bit of danger. Maybe they will think differently of me after they see me in action."

"You sound very sure of yourself," Taylor said. "It surprises me that you would say you are shy."

Josie smiled at him. For the first time in her life, she said something that was on her mind without thinking about it first. "I feel comfortable with you, Taylor. And please, do call me Josie."

"I will do that."

"Where are you staying right now?" Josie asked. "Do you have a place of residence that is permanent?"

"Yes," Taylor responded, nodding. She watched as he shifted his hat from one hand to the other. He had large strong-looking hands. She would feel safe whenever she was around him, that was for sure. He held a presence that was very striking. "I bought a large house with rooms for my children to play in, rooms for my mother and myself, a large house on Jetters street. Do you know where that is?"

Josie searched her mind but had no idea where the street he mentioned happened to be. She shook her head. "I'm afraid not, but as I said, I've been here about the same amount of time as you. When my sisters and I visited our uncle here while I was growing up, we really didn't do a lot of traveling around town. Even if we had, I wouldn't have noticed street names. I was too busy looking at pretty ribbons for sale at the general store."

"I do like it here in Sacramento," Taylor said, his voice suddenly wistful. "I think Becky would have enjoyed it as well. Beautiful sunsets, beautiful people."

Josie felt sympathy for him fill her chest. "You must miss her terribly."

He nodded. "I do. But I have accepted her death. I don't want to sound harsh, and I truly hope I don't. I loved her very much. But I have to live on. I couldn't let her death make me any less loving or attentive to my children. My mother has stepped into the role for my children, and that is a blessing to me. I may not have been able to get through without her help. I am sure, in fact, that I wouldn't have."

"I look forward to meeting her," Josie said. "I'm assuming she will want to have a part in our investigation?"

"Yes. She's the one who recommended you to me."

"Well, we are going to do our best for you," Josie said, pushing herself to her feet. "If you will excuse me for a few minutes, I'm going to see my sisters. We live in the back part of this house. I will fill them in on what you've told me and come back to you with their decision. I wouldn't worry. I believe they will want to take your case."

"Thank you."

He had stood up when she did, and she left him the room to go tell her sisters about their new client.

5

"You were a long time," Sadie said, coming from the kitchen sink back to the table and sliding into her seat. "Who was it?"

"It's a new client," Josie said, barely able to contain her excitement. "I think we should take the case. His wife was killed on a train, and he's been getting these threatening letters, and he's afraid for his family. They moved all the way from New York here to California to get away from the threats, but they've been found, and he's worried they will come after his mother or his children, who came with him." The words came rushing out as she hurried to the table and took her seat.

She leaned forward, her eyes sweeping across her sisters and Larson as she continued, "They never found out who murdered his wife, and even though he thinks the letters are somehow connected, he can't find a connection that proves it. The lawmen aren't taking it seriously enough for him, so he's decided to hire us to find out who is sending the letters and possibly who killed his wife."

She finished with little breath left in her lungs and sucked in air, her eyes wide as she took in the expressions on her sisters' faces.

Josie couldn't help noticing the look of pride on Adelaide's face. "You certainly didn't have any trouble assessing your first client," her oldest sister said with a firm nod. "What's his name? You did get that, didn't you?"

Josie chuckled with the rest of them, nodding. "Oh yes, I did. Taylor Jameson. His mother and two children live here with him in a big house he bought."

"How do you want to handle this one, Adelaide?" Sadie asked, turning her attention to their oldest sister. "Josie can run with this if she wants, don't you think?"

"I can't run with it," Josie protested immediately,

shaking her head. "I'm glad I was able to do what I did, but I can't handle an investigation on my own. I'm not skilled enough for that. I need help from one of you."

"You can do it," Sadie replied in an encouraging voice. "I have faith in you."

"No, she's right," Adelaide said, bringing the attention to herself. She gave Josie a gentle smile. "I'm glad you're enthusiastic about it and want to help, and I have faith in you, too, but you're right. You don't have enough experience, not yet anyway. I'll go along with you and guide the way. I do want you to take the lead, though, and I will just answer questions you might have and help with observations. Does that sound all right to you?"

Josie was comfortable with what her sister offered. She knew she wasn't ready for her own line of investigation. She was still learning and was positive her observational skills weren't nearly as good as her sisters. It was one of the reasons she and Belinda stayed in the office most of the time. They were good with books rather than picking out clues.

Josie hoped this investigation would prove different for her. Maybe it was time she spread her wings and flew.

The exciting thoughts in her head made her skin tingle.

"I wonder if he's eaten," Belinda said quietly.

Josie glanced at her sister, holding in a chuckle. She hadn't thought of that. She hadn't even offered him a drink. She felt like a bad hostess.

She got to her feet again. "I forgot to offer him some coffee or something. Oh, I'm terrible. I'll go make sure he doesn't want anything while you discuss it."

"There's no need for discussion," Adelaide said, also standing. She dropped her napkin on her empty plate, her eyes moving to Larson. "You'll be needed for this at some point, I'm sure. I'll want you to go with Josie wherever she goes to protect her from harm. I don't have to tell you your job."

Larson shook his head. "No, ma'am, you don't."

Adelaide nodded, a satisfied look on her face. She waved one hand at Josie, rotating her wrist several times. "Come along, Josie. Let's go talk to this Taylor Jameson and find out what he knows. I'm sure you jotted down a few notes as I told you to do last time, right?"

"I did," Josie replied, beaming at her sister. She felt like she'd accomplished something major.

"Good." The sound of approval Adelaide's voice

made Josie feel even more confident. "We'll be right back, sisters."

Following close behind Adelaide, Josie hurried down the corridor, back to the main office. As soon as she went in, she offered him a drink.

"We have coffee, tea, or something stronger if you like."

Josie noticed when she walked in that the look of worry on Taylor's face had deepened since she left. She wondered what he was thinking that made him look the way he did, deep and brooding. A moment of insecurity made her wonder if she'd said some-thing to put him off or make him think twice about hiring them.

"I wouldn't mind a cup of hot tea if you have some," Taylor replied. "I believe that might help soothe my nerves."

"I am Adelaide Salinger," Adelaide said, going to him with her arm extended. He grasped her hand, and they shook. "Is it all right if I call you Taylor?"

"Yes, that's fine."

Adelaide went to the other side of the desk and sat down. She glanced at the notepad with Josie's notes written on it and slid her eyes to the letters in their envelopes.

"She's told us your predicament," she stated,

picking up the three letters. "These are the letters you mentioned?"

"That's correct."

Josie took the seat across from the desk next to Taylor, where she'd been at the beginning of their conversation. She said nothing, watching as her sister opened the letters and read through them.

"No particular threat here. Just saying they will get you. That they want something." She lifted her eyes to Taylor. "What do they want?"

"I don't know," Taylor answered, sounding desperate. "That's where I'm having trouble. And that they want me to respond in the paper. I didn't understand what that meant until Josie said to put in an ad and she will go meet them."

Adelaide's eyes snapped to Josie's face. She could feel the blush in her cheeks and blinked at Adelaide.

"You offered to meet these men yourself? In Taylor's place?"

Josie nodded slowly, sliding her eyes to Taylor and back to her sister.

"Yes, I did," she said quietly.

"Well..." Adelaide looked like she didn't know what to say. "That's... brave of you." She returned her gaze to Taylor. "When you say you didn't know how to respond through the paper, is that because you don't know what they want?"

"I'm afraid if I go and they realize I don't know what they're talking about, they will kill me. I can't take that chance. I have children to think about. They've lost their mother. I can't let them grow up without their father, too."

Adelaide was quiet for a moment. Josie could tell she was thinking.

"If you are willing to meet these men in his place, I won't stop you," Adelaide said. "But you will need to have Larson somewhere nearby."

"I can keep watch, also," Taylor offered.

"No," Adelaide stated firmly. Both Josie and Taylor gave her a look of surprise. "You shouldn't be anywhere nearby. If you are seen, it could cause trouble, and someone might get hurt. It would be best for her to meet them with Larson present to keep her safe. She can be your representative to figure out what this is all about."

When Taylor looked at Josie, she felt a tingle slide through her body that she'd never felt in all her twenty-three years of life. She immediately chided herself, as he was a recent widower, and she had only known him for an hour. It was not the time for childish infatuations.

But his next words made that feeling hard to combat.

"I don't know if I want her to do that. No young woman should put their life on the line for me. Even if I do have children. It's not fair to ask her to do that."

6

Taylor hated the feeling of hopelessness that had been residing in his soul since the arrival of the first letter. He had nightmares that the criminals who had killed his wife would come after his children or his mother. The letters didn't make it any easier.

"I will be fine," Josie said, shaking her head. Her reassurance wasn't enough to make him feel much better.

"You aren't obligated to me in any way. No amount of money I pay would be worth risking your life over."

He could already tell that the woman was determined to do what she said—go meet with the criminals and negotiate a settlement. Maybe she was genuinely curious to know what it was they wanted. That was certainly a question on his mind. He'd been thinking about it for two years and still didn't know what they wanted.

"Taylor, tell me this," Adelaide said, getting his attention. "Why did you relocate after months of receiving the letters? It sounds like you are very based in New York. You have a lucrative business, many friends, a home, a life. Did something happen to make you move? A threat that scared you for your family?"

Taylor didn't want to think about it. Whenever he did, he had to relive it, and it was almost too much to bear. He drew in a breath and braced himself. He'd been lovingly scolded by Becky on many occasions because he was a man of many emotions.

"I think you will find that I am a man who loves his children more than anything in the world," he replied in a quiet voice. "Those children are every-thing to me. Yes, something did happen to make me leave. My children were being taught by a lovely young woman named Clara. She was their nanny, caregiver, and teacher. She was also Becky's best friend. She came to help with the children after Becky was taken. She was..." He hesitated, seeing the young woman's face in his mind, a deep sense of mourning passing through him. It was different than what he felt for his wife.

"Take your time, Taylor," Josie encouraged him softly.

He breathed heavily and continued, "She was killed. In her home a few months after my wife. There was no connection found between the two deaths, according to the lawmen that investigated. It appeared she was a victim of a burglary. She bravely fought back against the intruders, but they shot her."

"Oh my," Josie breathed, shaking her head.

"Since it didn't have anything to do with my family, the law didn't associate it with the threats we'd been getting."

Adelaide clucked her tongue in disapproval. "Utterly ridiculous. All angles must be looked at to find the truth. I'm assuming they didn't find out who shot her?"

"No. It was never solved. That was a year ago now, or close to it. We relocated immediately after that. I was afraid they were getting too close to my children."

"I hate to say it," Adelaide remarked, pushing the last of the letters back into its corresponding enve-lope, "but it surprises me that you, your children, and your mother have lasted this long safely. It sounds like they mean serious business."

Taylor sighed, the hopeless feeling washing over him again. "You don't know the measures I've taken to keep them safe. For a few months here in California, we lived free of fear and were able to move about without worry. Now we are back to the same routine we had in New York, hiding from the world, scared to go outside, scared to be without each other. I don't want a ton of servants doing everything and anything for us. We want to go and explore and see things and go to the beach and have fun like we used to. I am angry that my children are being put through this and angry that I feel like I'm the one doing it to them. I don't want to restrict them. I want them to run and play and have fun."

"Perfectly understandable," Adelaide said, nodding.

Josie jumped to her feet, her eyes wide, staring at Taylor. He lifted his eyebrows.

"I forgot your tea." Josie's face was as red as a beet. Taylor couldn't help being amused by her and gave her a small smile.

"It's perfectly all right. You were distracted."

"I was, but that's no excuse. Please don't go anywhere. I'll be right back."

She hurried from the room looking like a retreating rabbit, making Taylor hold in a chuckle. He looked at Adelaide.

"Your sister is quite a character. I like her."

"Thank you," Adelaide replied, smiling. "She can be quite the handful. But she's grown into a fine young woman. She has always been a very intuitive young lady but not very aggressive in the social department. I'm surprised she is so easy-going with you. You must have something special about you."

Taylor was surprised by the pleasant feeling that filled him, making him warm inside. "Flattery is such a nice thing," he quipped.

She grinned, letting out another light laugh. "It's nice that you are able to smile despite what you are going through."

Taylor grunted. "I have already been through so much associated with this I almost feel as though I'm becoming numb. I'm afraid for that to happen, though. If I cannot feel the worry, the fear, the concern, I'm afraid I will become complacent, and something will happen to someone I love. My children and mother are my number one concern. But of course, I must keep myself safe so that I don't leave them in this world to fend for themselves. I fear for my own safety only because they will be lost without me. It's my duty to take care of them. I failed in that regard when it comes to Becky. I will not make that mistake with my children."

Taylor swallowed the tears that were rising in his throat and cleared it just as Josie came back into the room with a cup and saucer in her hand, steam rising in wisps from the liquid.

"Here you go." She stopped short, staring at him. It was only a brief pause, but it made him wonder what she saw that made her react that way. Did he look that bad?

She handed him the cup, and he stared down into it, breathing in the scent of the tea.

"This smells very nice." He touched the small spoon and glanced around the cup at the three squares of sugar cubes sitting next to it.

"I can get milk if you want some," Josie said, hovering over her seat, waiting for his answer.

He looked up at her and shook his head. "No, this is perfect, thank you. I don't know how you knew I like three cubes." He plopped the sugar in the hot tea and stirred it with the provided spoon. She looked pleased as punch as she sat in the chair she'd abandoned.

"I think you can tell we are going to take the case, Taylor," Adelaide said in a confident voice. "Let's devise a plan and put it into action. We like to do things one step at a time and follow up on each clue as we find it, gathering as much information as we can and then piecing it all together. It may take some time, but I feel confident we can make some headway with this. Shall we put together a plan now?"

Taylor nodded, a spark of newfound positivity filling him. "Yes. Let's make a plan."

7

The office was quiet. Josie was alone, searching through some of the records her uncle had kept of the cases he'd worked. One case in particular had caught her eye.

She'd come into the office with the intention of finding out her uncle's methods of interrogation. What questions did he ask? How did he speak? Where did he conduct these question-and-answer sessions, and how did he get people to talk to him?

There had to be specific things he would say and do, rules he would follow. Josie didn't see how he could have had the success rate he had without a set of rules.

The case she'd found the most intriguing was actually a set of cases linked together by one murderer. Women were the victims of the crimes. Six, to be exact. The murders had all taken place between two California towns called Jeetersville and Barnstown, which were ninety and a hundred and ten miles from Sacramento, respectively.

Uncle Gabriel had kept many notes on the case as he interviewed people who had seen the victims last: husbands, beaus, fathers, mothers, so many people. Josie could tell by what he'd written the people were open to speak with him about their perished loved ones. They were all willing to give him their thoughts on who they suspected the killer might be. They had pondered among themselves who it could be and whether or not it was one solitary killer or several men doing the deed.

Despite the many people interviewed and questioned, the lawmen were unable to find the killer.

It wasn't until Uncle Gabriel took over the case that things started to fall into place. He pieced it together and discovered a gardener had worked for all of the victims at one time or another. After an eighteen-month killing spree, six women dead and countless lives damaged beyond repair, the killer was caught and hung shortly after being sentenced.

As intriguing as the overall case was, Josie's focus was on the interviews and how her uncle conducted them. As she fingered through a drawer filled with his writings, she stopped on a folder with thicker binding paper than the rest of the drawer's contents. She pulled it out and saw that it was actually bound together with a leather strip wound through holes on one side of the paper, creating a book of sorts.

She held it in front of her and scanned the front. She recognized her uncle's handwriting and was immediately interested in what was inside. On the front page, Uncle Gabriel had written a title in large letters.

Guide to Conducting Interviews

It was exactly what Josie was looking for. A memory suddenly flashed through her mind, wiping out what was in front of her eyes at that moment and replacing it with the office from years ago, when she was much younger.

"What you doing, Uncle Gabriel?" she heard herself asking in her ten-year-old voice.

"I'm writing a guide, Josie," her beloved uncle's voice followed her own, and grown-up Josie closed her eyes, relishing in the memory. "This is going to help me and anyone I might have come in and take over for me when I'm old and feeble. Maybe that will be you. Would you like that, my girl?"

"Oh, very much, Uncle Gabe," she had

exclaimed, bouncing on her toes and clapping her hands softly. "I want to be an investigator just like you."

"You will have to be very bold and brave to do what I do, Josie. Do you think you can be bold and brave?"

Josie remembered the apprehension she'd felt as a child, thinking about how important her uncle's job was and how much courage it would require—courage she didn't think she had at the time.

Josie came out of the memory, wondering if she had the courage *now*. She was afraid all the time. Afraid she would mess something up, forget something important, not see what was right in front of her. She was afraid to disappoint her sisters, make a mockery of their company or damage the reputation her uncle worked so hard to build for his agency.

She'd been hiding in the shadows for too long, though, and she knew it. Her sisters were the bold and brave ones her uncle was looking for. It would require work from her to be like them. Hard work. It would mean focusing and concentrating and not letting her mind wander.

It had been three days since they had placed the ad in the paper. They were still waiting to see one in response or for Taylor to receive a letter. She'd spent those three days going over all the documents Taylor brought her, the letters he'd received in New York, and reports written by police in the case of the death of his wife. There was a lot, but she did her best to absorb everything she could. She noticed the missing link between Becky's death and the mysterious letters.

It didn't seem logical that the letter-writers never mentioned what it was they were looking for. It was as if they assumed Taylor already knew. Did they think by not mentioning it, they would somehow be off the hook legally for committing a crime? It was still blackmail and threatening, even if they didn't mention the particular item they wanted. Josie found it hard to have respect for the criminals. She didn't think they were going about it in a smart way at all.

It had also crossed her mind that the two really *weren't* linked. Both the murder of his wife and the murder of her best friend, Clara, could have been coincidences and completely unrelated. New York wasn't a small town. Crime there was much more rampant than it would be in a smaller place with fewer people.

But Taylor seemed sure the letters had something to do with his wife. So sure, in fact, that Josie found it difficult to question the theory. When she met with the criminals and found out what they were looking for, it would go a long way to knowing the truth about that.

Her heart jumped when she thought about meeting them. It would have to be done in a public place. There was no way she was going to just invite them over to the house for a cozy dinner. There was an element of danger she was well aware of, but it wasn't going to stop her from trying.

She had to show her sisters she could be as bold and brave as her uncle wanted her to be.

She nearly jumped out of her skin when a loud knock sounded on the door outside. Whoever it was had to be aware of the second set of double doors and wanted to make sure they were heard. Why they didn't just push the bell was beyond her.

She got to her feet, setting the Guide to Conducting Interviews on the desk before leaving the main office and heading for the front doors.

When Josie pulled the door open, she looked up at Taylor and immediately thought how different he looked from their first meeting. It had been three days, and she had seen him only once in that time for a brief meeting to report nothing new.

His eyes were alight with energy. Before he even said anything, he held up an envelope.

"They've replied," he said in a breathless voice.

Josie was covered by a cool breeze. She shivered and ushered him in.

"Hurry," she said, "it's cold out there."

8

Taylor wasn't sure how to feel when Josie opened the door. He was excited that the criminals had written and were willing to set up a meeting with her as the respondent. The place they'd chosen was public—a popular restaurant for tourists and natives alike there in Sacramento. He knew of the place and was a little surprised they had chosen such a fancy restaurant to meet in. It required money to dine there.

On the other hand, as soon as he saw her face, he was reminded that she was going to meet them. Not him. She was small and pretty and probably easily breakable. He hated that she was going into the face of danger on his behalf.

When she told him to come in, he eagerly went

past her, wanting to get into the warmth of the offices within. He'd noticed on his two previous visits to the Wagon Wheel Justice offices how the women kept the place fairly cold. He wondered where they were from that made California weather warm enough to not stoke the fire as often. Being from New York, he was also tolerant to the cold more than some natives to the state.

Taylor hadn't asked any personal questions of the women, though he was beginning to wonder more and more about them. They got along better than any sisters he'd seen, especially considering there were four of them. They each seemed to have their own place in the system, Adelaide taking charge and assigning them all tasks, which they dutifully did. Their loyalty to each other was apparent, and Taylor valued that.

"Please read it to me," Josie said urgently, following him into the main office.

He already had the letter unfolded and looked up at her, saying, "Where are your sisters? Do they want to hear it, too?"

"They aren't here," Josie replied, moving closer to him, her eyes as curious as her voice. "They will read it later. Don't make me wait. Please." She smiled, and he felt a rush of warmth go through him.

Ignoring the feeling, he turned his attention to the paper and read it aloud.

"Your message in the paper was seen and understood. Meeting with a representative is accepted. Friday evening, seven pm, Count and Cordley."

Josie's eyebrows pulled together, and she gave him a questioning look. "Count and Cordley? What does that mean?"

"It's a restaurant," Taylor answered, surprised she didn't know about it. "You have never been there?"

Josie shook her head. "I've never even heard of it. One of my sisters might have. Though I doubt it. We have not done a great deal of dining at restaurants since we came to California."

Taylor couldn't keep the curious question from coming out. "Where are you and your sisters from?"

"We spent a good deal of time here growing up while visiting our uncle," Josie said, going to the desk and sitting behind it. Taylor sat across from her. "The rest of the time, we were in Virginia. When we grew up and weren't teenagers anymore, we got jobs and started living our lives and didn't come back nearly as often. We mostly corresponded with Uncle Gabriel through letters. We did a lot of writing. I kept all his letters."

Taylor could hear the affection she had for her

uncle in her tone of voice. That feeling was reflected by the look on her face as well.

"How long has it been since you lost your uncle?" he asked gently, hoping he wasn't overstepping his bounds. He was a client. Maybe she didn't want to discuss personal things with a client. He was curious, though, and she didn't seem to mind answering him.

"He's been gone coming up on a year. See, we actually came to Sacramento right after he passed because he left us the agency and already had a job for us lined up. I think he wanted to introduce us to it all right away. It was Adelaide that really took to it, of course. She's the smartest of us girls."

Taylor gave her a warm smile. "I'm sure you are just as smart as she is in your own way."

Josie nodded. "Yes, that's true. I have many qualities which may or may not be different from my sisters. So, in my own way, yes. But I'm not as smart as she is, and I'm willing to admit that."

Taylor lifted one hand and placed it firmly under his chin, narrowing his eyes at her. "I'm thinking I may need to get the smarter sister on this case."

Josie gasped but smiled wide when he laughed and shook his head.

"I'm kidding. I feel like I'm talking myself into a

corner so let's change the subject, shall we? Your uncle must have had great faith in all four of you to leave with such an awesome responsibility."

Josie looked thoughtful, her eyes roaming around the large office. "I suppose you could say it is an awesome responsibility. But I have welcomed it with open arms. We feel we have a purpose in life, and that is to help others in need. It may be dangerous, but someone has to do it, isn't that right?"

Taylor was impressed with her answer. He nodded, never taking his eyes from hers.

She was the one to drop her gaze first. She picked up a thick bound folder from the desk and held it up, shaking it in the air.

"I'm glad the meeting is for Friday. That gives me two days to read through this manual my uncle wrote on how to conduct interviews. If I fill my head with tips from him on how to behave and what questions to focus on, I think it should be easy. Well, maybe not easy but easier."

Taylor could picture Josie in the Count and Cordley but not for a dangerous meeting with his enemies. It would be so much better for her first experience there to be one of fun and romance. It was a shame the restaurant would be tied to this misadventure.

Still, he felt a little more secure that it was such a highbrow place. And she would have their bodyguard, Larson, there to protect her should anything untoward happen.

But what could possibly happen? They weren't after her. Their ad in the paper mentioned a meeting was requested to discuss the item in question. Not to give over the item. To discuss it. With a representative and not him.

He was glad they had agreed to it. It meant the end of the mystery was on the horizon. It might open up a whole new box of trouble, but at least he'd know what was being sought.

Progress had been made so quickly. He wished he had turned to the agency sooner, but it wasn't until his mother mentioned it that he even knew about it. He wondered if it would already be solved if he'd gone to an agency in New York when it all first started.

Taylor knew why he hadn't sought to start his own investigation. He had truly relied on the police force in New York to investigate and find the murderers. When they found no link between her death and the letters and threw their hands in the air with the case, that's when he'd moved to Sacramento, figuring there was no other way but to run.

He was done running.

"I'm glad he left you with something to help you," he said, pulling from his thoughts and focusing on her. "It is a little more comforting to know you are strengthening your skills. I still object to the fact that you're willing to go into danger for someone you barely know. But I'm glad you are. I do want you to know that. I think you're incredibly brave for doing this."

Josie's eyes settled on his face. He felt a tingle flow through his body.

"I don't feel brave very often," she said. "I don't feel brave right now. But I hope I do when the time comes to step into that restaurant. A public place is best, and I'm glad to have the meeting. I just need to make sure I'm asking the right questions. I'll be safe, though. Nothing is going to happen to me in that restaurant."

"I hope not," Taylor responded in a low voice. "I'll never forgive myself if something does."

9

Josie was touched by his concern for her. She'd convinced herself it was just a meeting, and she had nothing to worry about. What were the chances they would actually pull out a gun and shoot her in such a public place?

The two days between the letter's arrival and the day of the meeting passed like they never existed.

Josie was seated in the largest cushioned chair in the big office, her feet up on an ottoman, the Guide to Conducting Interviews open on her lap. She could hear her sisters discussing the plan behind her with Larson and Taylor. Every now and then, she'd read another paragraph in the book and study a point list Uncle Gabriel had made. She'd gotten some good tips from the book and had sent a grateful "thank you" to him in Heaven several times while reading it.

"Josie, are you listening?"

She looked across the room at Adelaide, who was seated behind the big desk.

"I'm sorry," Josie replied. "I was thinking."

"It's okay. I understand. We were just discussing where we will be. Larson and I. We will be nearby. I'm also going so I can hear everything firsthand."

Josie understood why her oldest sister wanted to hear everything for herself. It only made sense that she was able to process everything through her sharp mind without the hindrance of receiving someone else's interpretation of what was said.

"We went and inspected the restaurant yesterday," Adelaide went on. "And chose the tables that will be used. I went ahead and spoke to the host. He is aware that we will need to be seated as close to the table that is chosen for you as possible."

Josie lifted her eyebrows. "How much did you tell him about what's going on?" She didn't mind if he knew more than he probably should. That just meant he'd be looking out for her, too.

"Not a lot. Just that you are an important figure, and we need to make sure you are safe with the men you are meeting with. He understood though I think he was surprised to be taking these directions from me instead of Larson."

Larson snorted. "He didn't seem to understand the concept of me working for you, which is dumb, in my mind. Lots of important women have employed bodyguards before. Queens and dignitaries in every country have men guarding women."

"Times are changing," Sadie spoke up, reaching out to pat her man gently on the cheek. "Someday, working for a woman won't be such a rare thing. I'm sure of it."

Adelaide cut into the casual conversation with a stern voice. "Make sure you are always on your guard and watch their movements to see if they have a hidden weapon. Don't let either of them touch you if you can avoid it."

"They aren't going to kill me with their fingertips, sister dear," Josie said with a soft laugh. "But I will be careful, I promise you. I don't want to get hurt."

"I don't want you hurt either. That's why we're going to be right there, watching and listening. There's always a risk, though, so I need you to be as careful as you can possibly be."

Josie nodded, hearing the seriousness of her sister's tone.

"I know you don't want me to be there," Taylor said and raised his hand when Adelaide drew in a breath, opening her mouth to speak. She shut it and allowed him to continue, "but I'm at least going to be waiting outside. I will watch from afar, and when they leave, I will be there outside, waiting for you. You come out and tell me everything. Can we at least agree on that?"

"Yes," Josie said, moving her eyes to Adelaide. She knew she would feel more comfortable knowing he was outside. His presence, along with Larson's and Adelaide's, sounded like complete protection from all sides to her. "What do you think, Adelaide?"

"If you would like to do that, I have no objection. You may find it to be a chilly night, though, standing outside waiting. What if it snows?"

"I will be very miserable if it snows in the next five hours," Taylor quipped, "especially since it's been a warm day all day and snow was not predicted in the almanac."

"All right, all right," Adelaide responded, soft laughter behind her words. "You're right. I was just giving you a little warning that it might make for an uncomfortable few hours."

"Oh, I hope it doesn't last that long," Josie moaned. "I want it to be quick and easy. I want to get it over with. I'll go in, sit down, and say what it is you want, and they will tell me, and I will leave." She let out a single chuckle. "Wouldn't that be perfect?"

"It would. I doubt it will be that fast, though." Taylor shook his head. "If it were that easy, they would have just proposed a meeting in one of the other letters. But they insisted on the message in the paper. I don't understand why."

"Hiding their tracks, perhaps?" Adelaide suggested, lifting her dark eyebrows. "Leaving a confusing trail, so it's hard to find them?"

"They wouldn't have suggested a meeting without knowing they have your attention, though," Josie said. "You might not show up if they just sent you a time and place."

"It's all a complete mystery to me," Taylor responded. "Two years of torment at a time when I was already distracted by pain and mourning. I feel a bit of a fool for not doing something sooner. But the letters were so sporadic. At first, I dismissed them, thinking they were a prank. But when Clara died, it became clear they were after me."

"There's still no real link between their deaths, though," Josie said what he probably didn't want to hear. She had gone through the newspaper articles written about both murders and the police records for both and had found nothing to link them together. The women hadn't died in the same way nor under the same circumstances. Becky was strangled while Clara was shot. Becky was on a train while Clara was at home. No notes or clues had been found that made the two events similar in any way. Only that they were friends. It was the only link.

"That's true," Taylor gave her a nod with his response, "but I know there's a connection. I just know it. I can feel it. In here." He tapped his chest with the tips of the fingers of one hand. He pulled in a deep breath. "I'm glad you are willing to help me find the truth." He swept his eyes over them all. "It means a lot to me. The safety of my children is more important than anything else. I cannot let anything happen to them. I wish I was there with them every minute of every day to keep them safe."

Josie looked at her sisters, unsure how to respond to his words. It was obvious how deeply he meant them. She admired his passion for being a father. He took the role very seriously. He was the kind of man she wanted the father of her own children to be. Fiercely protective and unconditionally loving. In just three encounters, she could tell that was Taylor in a nutshell.

She could only dream of finding a man such as

him to love and cherish and be loved and cherished by.

He turned his eyes to her and caught her staring at him. She was sure a look of pure admiration had to be on her face, and she quickly dropped her eyes, her cheeks flushing.

"Are you sure you want to do this, Josie?" he asked.

"I'm sure, Taylor," she responded, lifting her eyes and gazing directly at him. She wasn't going to show her frailty or fear. She was going to stand up and be brave, the way her uncle wanted her to be. She would show them all that she could be that woman, more like her sisters than she'd ever been before.

10

Josie's nerves were on the very edge. She was just able to keep herself from shaking like a leaf as she followed the host to the table that was reserved for her and her party. She slid into the chair and thanked the host, nodding when he asked if she would like a glass of wine while she waited for her companions.

"Red or white?" she was asked.

"White," she heard herself say.

She swallowed hard, looking around the room. It was difficult to see the tables around her, as they were formed in a t shape, and on each ledge in between each table were live potted plants, small bushes that blocked the view from or to any of the other tables.

She moved her eyes away from the front door, which she could just see, when her sister and Larson came in. They passed her by, but she didn't acknowledge them, and they didn't acknowledge her. They were seated to her right. She took some comfort in knowing they were there. She wanted desperately to whisper through the obstructing bush to see if her sister would respond. It would almost be like when they were children, whispering "secrets" through the bushes in the garden, playing one of their favorite games.

The four sisters would run around the garden, whispering made-up "secrets," which they would then have to repeat to a different sister exactly the same. Yet, the story was never the same when it got back to the first sister.

Remembering the game, Josie felt a sense of nostalgia pass through her. She kept herself from whispering through the bush, just in case there were other ears nearby, waiting for her to slip up.

After being seated for about ten minutes and having consumed her first few sips of white wine, Josie's heart nearly stopped when she saw two men enter the restaurant. They looked completely out of place. Even tourists did not dress the way they were dressed. They had to be from out of town.

They were average in size and stature, one slightly taller than the other but not notably tall. They wore big hats, which they pulled from their heads as soon as they entered, revealing opposite hair colors, the tall one dark brown and the slightly shorter one bright blond.

They both looked directly at her.

Her nerves seized, and her body became so tense it was painful. She forced herself to relax. She was perfectly safe, she told herself. Everything was going to be just fine. They weren't there to kill her. They were there to find out where their item was and to tell her what it was, too.

They walked to her table behind the host and thanked him, both ordering from the wine list in detail. Josie wondered if they'd been there before.

"You are the representative we are to meet?" the blond-haired man asked her, his voice low.

Josie hoped they would speak loud enough for her sister and Larson to hear.

"That's right," she said, louder than he was speaking but not loud enough to draw any attention. She wanted to sound confident, not arrogant.

"This meeting has been a long time coming," the blond one continued, "What has taken Mr. Jameson so long to contact us?"

"He doesn't know why you are contacting him," Josie responded. "I have read the letters, and you have never mentioned what it is specifically you wish for him to hand over to you. Additionally, there is nothing that he is aware he owes anyone, so there is no reason for him to comply with your wishes."

"We want the least amount of trouble possible," the fair-haired one said, leaning toward her. Both his hands were above the table, which gave Josie a bit of relief. The other man was sitting in a similar fashion, his hands folded together on the table in front of him. His dark eyes looked intense as he stared at her. If he was trying to intimidate her, he was doing a good job.

Still, she managed to keep herself from trembling while they spoke, and she counted that as an accomplishment.

"Then tell me what it is you seek, and I'll pass the message to him. If he has what you want and you present a good reason why he should give it to you, I'm sure he will do so. He is a man of honor and dignity. He keeps his word."

The two men looked at each other. Josie wondered what message they were passing with their eyes. The blond was the one who moved first, sitting back and putting one hand in his jacket. He pulled out a photograph and tossed it on the table in front of her.

"This is what we are seeking."

Josie looked down at the photograph. Even though there was no color, she could see the beauty and rarity of the necklace portrayed there. She noticed there was a second photograph under the first and pushed the top one to the side. The second portrayed a beautiful woman dressed in princess garb, wearing the necklace around her elegant neck. She wore a crown of similar design, and Josie was willing to bet the gems were the same colors.

"This is what you want?" she asked. "Why don't you offer to buy it from him? Why are you threatening him and his family for this?"

"You do not need to know what motivates us," the blond said in an almost growling sort of way. Josie wondered what she'd said that irritated him. He seemed to be angry for no reason. "This necklace is ours. Mr. Jameson has the necklace and will deliver it to us at our next meeting."

"I can't guarantee that," Josie surprised herself by stating the words with conviction. "I have to talk to him first. He might not even know where this necklace is."

The dark-haired man finally spoke up, leaning

forward and giving her a menacing look. "You will want to encourage him to find it if he doesn't know where it is. Our patience had grown thin. He has good timing approaching us now. We were at the end of the rope, and on the verge of making a move he does not want us to make."

Josie's stomach erupted in cramps with anxiety. She worked hard not to cringe and give herself away. She stared hard at the dark-haired man, hoping she wasn't showing her fear. He had a strange accent that could only subtly be heard in his voice. She wondered where he was from originally.

The blond man lifted a hand in the air as if to tell the dark-haired man to be quiet. Josie knew who was in charge after the second man shut his mouth and sat back again.

"We will be watching for another message in the newspaper. When the necklace is found, contact us. We will send a letter with instructions."

"You will need to give him a good reason to give you the necklace. You can't just threaten him repeatedly. If you tell him why he might cooperate with you."

"It is for us to know why, Miss, and for you to tell him to find the necklace. Many bad things have happened to innocent people because of his negligence and ignorance."

"What innocent people have you hurt?" The words burst out. She was once again surprised by her courage. "Are you talking about Becky? Clara? Are they your victims?"

The men shared another glance but stood up instead of responding.

"Place the ad in the paper when the necklace is ready for pickup," the blond man repeated the instructions, keeping his voice low, his eyes flicking around the restaurant. For a moment, Josie was afraid they would see Larson and Adelaide and somehow recognize them.

"We will send you a letter. Do this soon so that no one else is hurt," the man said, and both turned and left Josie breathing heavily at the table.

11

───────

As soon as he saw the men leave the restaurant, Taylor moved along the side of the building and slipped in through the entrance. He saw Josie, rooted in her chair at the table, her eyes wide, staring down at the table in front of her. He followed her eyes and saw what looked like a photograph. He hurried over and saw that it was, in fact, two photographs.

"Josie," he hissed, drawing her from her stupor. Her naturally narrow violet eyes flipped up to him. She hopped out of the chair and surprised him by grabbing both his arms and squeezing.

"Taylor. It's a necklace. They want a necklace. Do you really think someone would kill for a piece of jewelry? Is that really done?"

At first, he wasn't sure what to say. Did she expect a real answer from him, or was that a rhetorical question?

Before he could say anything, though, Adelaide was behind Josie, reaching out to pull her into a hug.

"You did wonderfully, Josie," Adelaide was saying, her voice low but encouraging. "I'm so proud of you. I'm going to tell the sisters how brave you were. You really surprised me. Good job, my dear."

"Thanks, Adelaide." Josie seemed to calm down as Adelaide hugged her tight. Taylor was still reeling from the way she'd grabbed onto him. While her sister comforted her, he picked up the photographs, and a jolt of recognition split through him.

"This is what they want? This necklace?" He was a little confused. He recalled when he'd been given the necklace. He was a boy, to be sure, and it was jewelry handed down from when his family had been royalty. Dukes and earls. The titles had faded, and though they were still used sometimes, they held no real place in American society. So the jewelry had been sent down through the generations, and he ended up with one of the rarer pieces. It was worth a good deal of money—but not enough to take someone's life, surely.

Two lives, for that matter, if his theories were correct.

"Do you recognize it?" Josie asked, pulling away from her sister.

Taylor nodded. Without taking his eyes from the photograph of the woman wearing the jewelry, he slid into a seat. The others followed suit.

"It's a family heirloom. I gave it to my wife. To Becky, just after we were married. I remember her joking that there wouldn't be a ball grand enough for her to wear it to and that she would probably keep it locked away for safety reasons. I don't think I ever saw her wear it. This..." He tapped the photograph with one finger, "looks like a photograph of my ancestor, Princess Lavinia Rose Cardingale, who was actually in charge of an entire island when she was just a girl of fifteen. She ruled the land until she was twenty, when there was a revolution, and she was murdered. The rival faction took over for a time, and the necklace was one of the items used in payment for ransom about fifty years later."

"My goodness," Josie exclaimed breathlessly, her eyes wide and intrigued. He felt a sense of pride slip through him, making him smile at her. "That's an amazing story."

"I actually just remembered it, seeing this photo-graph," Taylor replied, dropping his eyes to the rendition on thick paper. "I used to wish she would wear it—Becky, of course. Just so I could see it some-times. But then I forgot about it. I guess she locked it away. Once it was out of my sight, I never thought of it again. Until now, of course."

"That's what they want." Josie sounded flabber-gasted when she spoke the words.

Taylor understood her confusion.

"Why do they want it? What makes them think I should just hand it over to them? If that was the way of the world, everyone everywhere would be threat-ening each other that if they aren't given what they want, they'll start killing people. That's holding everyone hostage. I'm not just going to give in. What about Becky? Did you get anything on that?"

Josie shook her head, which disappointed him, but he felt a little better when she said, "No, but they did say that innocent people have suffered because you didn't immediately give them the necklace."

"I didn't know that's what they wanted. Becky was killed before the letters started coming. Was she going to give it to them? If she was, why would she do that?"

Taylor's own questions were leading him down a

path he didn't want to go on. What if Becky had been doing something behind his back? What if she was making shady deals and moving in circles she had no business being in? Men weren't the only corrupt beings on the planet. Plenty of women had their hand in the pot, as well.

"Don't start doubting your wife until you have more facts to go on," Adelaide said in warning. "The first thing you need to do is get the necklace. Do you know where it is?"

Taylor had to think about it. They had moved. The necklace could have been anywhere. It might even still be in New York, in a security box somewhere, or tucked away in a bank vault.

He shook his head. "No. I have no idea where it is. My wife's jewelry... I suppose we could go through the boxes we brought with us. I didn't bring all her things, but her jewelry and valuable possessions are going to our daughter, so I brought them to Sacramento with us, in case we never returned to New York."

"So you have her jewelry here then?"

"Yes, it would be at the house right now. We could go look through it if you like."

Taylor glanced around the table at Larson and Adelaide, who were both nodding their heads.

"I think that's a good idea, Josie," Adelaide said, sounding a bit like a superior rather than a sister. Josie didn't seem to take offense, though. She just nodded.

"I don't see why not. But maybe first we could get something to eat? I'm so hungry, and it smells so good in this place."

Taylor's stomach had grumbled from the moment he stepped into the restaurant, so he heartily agreed with Josie. He sat forward, drawing attention to himself. "I tell you, I could use some good food. Just something quick, and then we'll head back to the house and search through Becky's things for this necklace."

For an hour, Taylor relaxed with the two sisters and their bodyguard, eating and enjoying their chatter. He couldn't help noticing how the two sisters complimented each other, smiled often, and behaved in a friendly, cordial fashion. They were made of fine stock, he decided, and it was worth his time and money hiring them to solve his mystery.

By the time they left, he was wishing he'd come with them in their buggy instead of riding his own horse, so he could have spent a little extra time talking to Josie on the ride. But he was on his own horse, riding alongside the buggy, listening to their conversation and feeling like an outsider.

He was glad when they got to his house.

That is, until he got out of the saddle and went up on his front porch.

12

There was still enough light for Josie to see why Taylor was so upset when he went to the front door of his house. It wasn't all the way closed.

She shared a worried look with Adelaide, grabbing her skirt as soon as she was on the ground and going up the steps carefully. Her heart was immediately knocking in her chest. Taylor's mother and children should have been in that house. The door should have been closed. The security measures Taylor had put into place to keep his family safe seemed all for naught.

He burst through the door and immediately called for his mother.

"Mother," he cried out, his head swiveling from

one direction to the other. "Bella. Alex. Papa's home. Come to Papa. Where are you?"

He ran to the door of the parlor and pushed it open all the way. When he cried out in dismay, Josie moved her eyes beyond him and saw an overturned table in the room. She went to his side and looked around him at the devastation. It looked like a tornado had gone through.

"What is going on? Who is doing this?"

"They came looking for the necklace while we were at the restaurant," Adelaide breathed. Josie could hear the underlying anger in her voice. "I don't believe it."

"Where is my mother?" Taylor turned to Adelaide, spitting out the words as if Adelaide had the answers. "Where are my children? Where are they?"

He took off, going from one room to another and then bolting up the stairs. Josie understood why he was so terrified. She felt like she might faint herself, and she hadn't even met the children. She went up the stairs after him and found him motionless in the children's playroom. He was holding a rag doll, a look of complete devastation on his face.

He turned to her, and when he spoke, his voice

was so deep and low she had to move closer to hear him.

"I didn't keep them safe. This is my fault. No matter how hard I tried, I couldn't keep them safe."

"We need to get to the agency and notify the sheriff, Taylor. A search needs to be put underway. We'll form our own posse and search the streets and the woods and the plains beyond. We'll find them, Taylor, I swear it."

Taylor shook his head. "I can't go anywhere. What if they come back and there's no one here to protect them?"

"They left the fire burning," Josie said with more confidence than she felt. "They will be hiding out somewhere if they aren't hiding in this house. Let's check the cellar. There are still plenty of places they might be. Don't worry. Everything will be all right."

Josie knew full well the chances of everything being all right were slim. She tried not to see the look of despair Taylor cast her way. He didn't believe a word she was saying.

"Let's check the cellar," he said, bolting out of the playroom, still clutching the rag doll. Josie followed closely behind him. They went down the stairs and rounded the corner, Taylor in the lead, but both came to an abrupt halt when Adelaide and Larson emerged from the cellar door.

Taylor grunted with frustration and put hands on the sides of his head. "This can't be happening. My wife, now my children, my mother. This can't be happening. Not because of a necklace. I've been cursed. That's what it is. I've been cursed by the Devil."

Josie couldn't imagine the pain he was feeling. She wanted to comfort him, but what could she say? She was aware of the security measures he'd put into place to try to keep his family safe. There were many locks on the doors. The windows were always closed and locked. The children never went anywhere alone. He'd told Josie his next move would have been to get several large, loud dogs.

She wished he'd already done that.

"It's getting dark," she said, using a gentle tone. "We should start lighting some lanterns. We won't be able to see them if they are hiding once it's dark. We should check outside. Surely you have some outer buildings where they might be."

Taylor shook his head. "They won't hide out there. My mother wouldn't allow something like that. She would do something smart. If... if she was able to do anything at all."

Josie's chest tightened with anxiety. "Don't think like that. We have to stay positive. Should we go tell the sheriff?"

"Yes," Adelaide said, turning to Larson. "You go tell the sheriff. Tell him to meet us at the agency. He can send whoever he needs to here so they can survey the damage, but I think the best thing we can do is go to the agency and form a plan of action. Obviously, we're going to want to get some men together as soon as possible to start a search."

She looked at Taylor with intense eyes. "When were you here last?"

"I left at 6:30 to go to the restaurant," Taylor replied.

"And they were here then?"

"Yes."

Josie watched the exchange between her sister and Taylor. She tried to deny that she was actually terrified to her very core but denying it didn't stop it from being true. The children... so small... so innocent. What had they done to deserve this? The fact that anyone could do this much damage and cause this much pain over a necklace... she couldn't fathom it. There had to be something more. There had to be a better reason.

"So it has been three hours since you saw them.

If they were taken from here in a buggy or a wagon, they could be... could be very far, but if they are on foot, they won't have gotten too far. I don't imagine the attack happened immediately after you left." Adelaide turned to look at Larson, who was standing by her side listening. "What are you doing? Off you go, Larson, go fetch the sheriff."

"Oh, yes." Larson jumped as if he'd been in a daze, turned, and dashed through the front door. Moments later, they heard his horse thundering down the road, fading as he moved into the distance.

"We should go to the agency," Adelaide repeated, her eyes back on Taylor. "I know you're worried, but the sheriff will be back here with deputies before long, so if your children do find their way back, they will be all right. They'll be found. You aren't really safe here, are you? Do you think they found the necklace?"

Taylor looked thoughtful. Josie watched his face as he went through several emotions while standing there in front of her.

Finally, he moved swiftly across the foyer and down the hall. He unhooked a lantern from a wall and lit it before proceeding down the corridor. He went through a doorway, and when she followed behind, Josie saw that it was a study. He went to a small closet in the corner and opened the door to reveal a very narrow space that seemed almost not worth the bother of being called a closet. There was enough room, however, for four long narrow wooden boxes stacked on top of each other.

Along the side of each was one word. "Becky."

He set the lantern down on the floor and hefted the boxes out, one by one, and lined them up on the floor. "Her jewelry is in one of these," he said. Josie could hear the pain in his voice. It made her heart hurt.

With an aggression Josie hadn't seen in him before, he put his fingers under the lids of each box and ripped the top off until he got to the third one. When he pulled the lid off, the light from the lantern made the contents sparkle.

He held his hand out to the box. "There. That's everything she had."

Josie went to the box and knelt before it. Adelaide did the same on the other side, and they stared into the box, where earrings, necklaces, and bracelets were lined up on soft velvet fabric, several layers stacked upon each other. Josie reached in and grasped the edges of the left and right sides of the fabric. She pulled off the top layer and stared at the jewelry underneath.

Josie did this four times before she got to the bottom of the box. The last piece of jewelry, which was all on its own, was a triple-layered pearl necklace. Josie fingered the pearls, fascinated by their beauty.

"Your wife had some lovely pieces," Adelaide complimented Taylor, who was still standing in the same spot, his red face turned away from the boxes of memories. Josie felt sympathy sweep through her.

"I didn't see the necklace in question," she said hurriedly, moving to replace the layers of jewelry into the box. "Let's get to the agency before the sheriff gets there. You're right, Adelaide. We do need to make a plan."

She replaced the lids of the boxes by just setting them where they belonged, grabbed Taylor's hand, and pulled him from the room. She saw the look of utter amazement on her sister's face, but that didn't matter to her.

It wasn't the time for delays. It was the time for action.

13

delaide wasn't the only one surprised by Josie's sudden aggression. Taylor was caught off guard by it as well. He had been sinking into a pit of despair, his heart aching for his children, and she'd pulled him out of it by grabbing at him.

She aggressively pulled him toward the front door. He glanced behind him to see Adelaide grab the lantern and follow them.

"We need to get to the agency," Josie was muttering as if the idea was their only saving grace. He ran his eyes around the grounds as soon as they were outside, quickly considering whether he wanted to do a search through the outbuildings like Josie had suggested. But he was sure his mother wouldn't have had his two children out in the cold, shivering in the dark, waiting for... what? Who?

A gust of cold wind blew past his face, reminding him that his initial thoughts had to be correct. His mother wouldn't have them outside. She would have found a warm, dry shelter.

This was assuming that they hadn't been snatched from the home and taken away to be held for ransom. If that was the case, he would gladly give up the necklace.

If he ever found it.

The thoughts in his mind terrified him. He wasn't the type of man who gave in to fear easily. But this was the biggest fear he had, and it had become a reality.

He fought tears, choosing to ride in the agency buggy with the ladies, knowing they wouldn't do him any good and would only serve to make him look weak. Now was not the time for weakness.

The three got down from the buggy one by one outside the agency. Taylor was about to go in when swinging lights and the sound of horses' hooves got his attention. He turned to see a deputy and Larson coming up to the building. Adelaide turned to wait for them, but Josie grabbed his hand and pulled him inside.

"It's too cold to be out there waiting. They'll be in shortly. Come on. Let's go find Belinda and Sadie."

They passed through the second set of double doors, and Josie led him across the central area to the door that led to their house in the back of the building.

As soon as she pulled the door open, Taylor breathed in the smell of freshly baked bread. He moved swiftly behind Josie down the hallway and emerged on the other side to hear a familiar sound coming from the kitchen.

It was a sound that filled his heart with joy and made him leap into action. He passed Josie with three long steps and burst through into the dining area to see his children, his mother, and Sadie sitting at the table enjoying hot cocoa with marshmallows.

"Papa," Bella cried out, hopping down from the chair she'd been perched on. She ran to him and threw her arms around his waist, pressing herself against him.

Taylor felt like he could barely breathe. His mother and Alex also came to him, holding out their arms for hugs. Taylor bent and picked Alex up, putting one arm around his mother's shoulders.

"I can't believe it," he gushed, pressing a kiss against his mother's white hair. "I was thinking the worst. How... how did you come to be here? What is going on? What happened? You are all okay? Safe and sound?"

"Safe and sound, Taylor," his mother replied, nodding, her eyes softening when she looked at him. "It was very frightening, but if it wasn't for my excellent hearing, we might not have gotten out of there. God bless. It was a miracle."

"Come and sit down and tell us what happened. Please." Josie held her hands out to the table they'd just left, and they all gathered around it. Taylor sat in one of the chairs but continued to hold his son, who was now resting his head against Taylor's shoulder. He was reminded how late it was.

"Before you tell us the story, Mother, maybe we should fit these children into a bed somewhere. It's getting late, and I know Alex here doesn't want to hear any scary stories before bed, do you, son?"

"No, Papa," Alex's weary voice mumbled into his shoulder.

"Of course, of course." It was Josie who jumped up, holding her arms out to Bella. Taylor was astonished to see his daughter, who was friendly but cautious, go right to her. She put her hand in Josie's and allowed herself to be led out of the room without even a glance back at her grandmother or father.

Taylor shared a warm look with his mother before standing up and following Josie out of the room.

He saw her go through a doorway and went in behind her, stopping just on the other side. It was as though the room was made for the children to stay in. One bed was decorated with a bright pink quilt. The other was blue. Two small nightstands with two candles in brass holders that Josie lit to cast soft light throughout the room.

"This is a spare room," Josie said quietly. She lifted Bella onto one of the beds and began to remove her little boots. "You don't mind sleeping in your underclothes, do you, Bella?"

The little girl shook her head. Taylor saw the way his daughter stared at Josie with a fascinated expression on her face. He would be hearing more about Josie in the future, he could already tell. She would probably think Josie was a princess and, therefore, should be treated with great reverence.

Taylor went to the blue bed and laid Alex down after pulling back the quilt. He removed the boy's shoes and tucked him under the blankets. Alex snuggled into the thick pillow, his eyes already closed, his breathing steady.

When he turned back and saw that Josie was perched on the edge of the bed, brushing Bella's blond hair from her forehead, he got a rush of emotion that almost made him weak in the knees. She was looking at his daughter the way Becky had when they had put the children to bed together.

And Bella was looking back with the same expression.

A feeling of guilt swept through him. Becky couldn't be replaced. But he had professed he was moving on with his life, hadn't he? Was it wrong to develop feelings for another woman? To be attracted to her because she showed strong motherly traits? What if that was all he was looking at? Maybe she was horrible in other ways.

Taylor held in the grunt that wanted to come out. Looking at Josie, he couldn't see a single flaw. She was confident, beautiful, kind, intelligent... what more could a man want?

Josie leaned and pressed a kiss on the girl's forehead. "Sleep tight, Bella," she whispered, "and don't you worry. You are safe here."

She tapped the girl on the end of her nose, making her smile.

Taylor's heart took a leap in his chest. There was no way he would be able to see Josie any differently from that point on. She had grabbed his attention. When all this was over, he intended to do something about it.

14

When Josie and Taylor returned to the dining area, they were surprised to see Julia looking distraught, her eyes on the photographs Adelaide had laid out on the table. She looked up at her son, tears standing in her eyes. The deputy sat with the others, not interfering or asking any questions.

"Oh, Taylor," she wailed softly, "I am so sorry. I wish I had known. If I had known, maybe... maybe none of this would have happened."

Josie rushed to the table to sit near the older woman, though Taylor was the one who comforted Julia. He sat next to her and took both her hands in his, looking her directly in the eye.

"What do you mean, Mama?"

It was the first time Josie had heard him call his mother that. He had used the more formal "Mother" every other time he addressed the woman or even spoke of her. She sensed a hardness in his tone and wondered if he knew it was detectable.

She herself was curious. What did Julia know? How was she responsible for what had happened? Was she talking about the letters or her daughter-in-law's death? Or both?

"Mama, take a deep breath and talk to me."

Julia was panting, one hand pressed against her chest, the other against one temple. Her eyes were closed.

"This necklace. Adelaide says it is the object the letters are about. I... I didn't know, Taylor. I'm sorry."

"Where is the necklace, Mama?" Taylor asked. Josie could tell he was keeping himself under control. "Do you know where it is?"

Josie felt the same despair Taylor must have felt when his mother shook her head. "I... I don't know if it's where it's supposed to be or not. I... I thought Becky took care of all that."

A chill flashed over Josie's body, and her eyes flipped to Taylor. She was afraid he was going to find out something about his late wife he didn't want to know. From the look on his face, she could tell he suspected the same thing.

"What was Becky doing?" he asked in a barely audible tone. "What was she doing? Where is the necklace?"

"It all started the year before... before she died," Julia said, her voice quiet. "You and the children were preparing for... it was a birthday party. It was Alex's second birthday party, and you were... you were bathing them. I believe that's when it was. Do you remember that?"

Taylor nodded slowly, his eyes never leaving his mother's face.

"I was in the kitchen preparing some of the food, cutting up cheese for the children, getting the cake ready... and there was a knock on the door. I answered it, and the man gave me a letter for Becky. It was thick and heavy. I could tell there was something in there besides paper. I took it to her, and she opened it right there in front of me. She didn't expect what she found. I could tell by the surprise on her face. It was this necklace." She pointed at the photograph. "Only it wasn't."

Taylor frowned. Josie caught a look from him and shook her head. He looked back at his mother.

"What do you mean, it wasn't?" he inquired.

"I said it was beautiful, and she said it was a fake. It was a copy of the one from our ancestors."

The room took on a sudden chill. Josie stared at the woman, fascinated by her story.

"A copy?" Taylor repeated. "Why did she have a copy made?"

"She... she didn't say... not specifically. She said she wanted to keep it safe in case anyone tried to steal it. I thought it was a good idea at the time. I never thought about it again."

"She didn't say why she had the copy made? Just that she wanted to keep it safe?" Taylor sounded unhappy by the revelation. Josie had to admit, it was helpful but really only opened up a whole new barrel of questions.

"Yes. That's all she said. And that it was a perfect copy. She marveled over how similar it was to the real thing."

"Are you *sure* it was *this* necklace?" Adelaide asked, pointing at the photograph, moving her finger around specific points of the representation. "This particular necklace? You couldn't be mistaken? That was several years ago."

Julia shook her head. "No, this is the necklace. It's part of a set. The crown that you see here. It's the other half with this necklace. It was lost long, long ago, and I doubt it will ever be found."

"And you have no idea where it would be now? The fake or the real one?"

"I don't know what she did with the fake one. The real one was in the family bank vault in New York. As far as I know, it's still there."

"That's not a good thing," Taylor surmised, his voice filled with regret. Josie had to agree. How would they bargain for their lives with a piece of jewelry that was over three thousand miles away?

"There's something I don't understand," she said, turning her body toward the table, so she was facing Adelaide. "They are threatening your family for the necklace, may or may not have had something to do with two deaths and expect you to hand them the necklace because they want it, or they will do what? Kill someone else? Doesn't it seem like they are playing all their cards right now? Too soon for them to be effective?"

She looked around at her sisters, who were staring at her in surprise.

She stared right back. "I'm just trying to say they seem to be getting desperate."

"They first sent letters nearly two years ago," Taylor said in a firm voice. "I ignored them. If I was them, I'd be getting desperate too. And angry along with it."

Sadie lifted her eyebrows. "It almost sounds like you condone what he's doing. Or admire it, at least."

Taylor shook his head. "Don't condone, admire, or respect it. I'm also saying I simply don't care whether I make them desperate or angry. They were already my enemy. I'm not going to be nice to them for the sake of it. I will turn the other cheek, but I won't be browbeaten into submission."

Josie wondered silently what would have happened if the bad men had gotten their hands on Taylor's family.

"How did they get in the house?" she asked Julia. The older woman turned her eyes to meet hers.

"They got in through the back door. I don't know how it was left unlocked. Or if it was. Maybe they found a way around the locks. I didn't hear any windows smashing. I never thought if I had to run from my home, it would be through the front door. My first thought was that when Taylor got home, he would know something had happened, and he would panic. I knew he would be with you, Josie, and so I came here, knowing it would be the first place you went."

"Why didn't you go to the sheriff's office?" Sadie

asked, a hint of curiosity in her tone.

"They haven't been helpful in this so far." Josie heard the subtle disdain in Julia's voice. "I wasn't going to put the safety of my grandchildren in their hands. I imagine they would have said I was hearing things and sent us home with no questions."

Josie looked over her shoulder at the deputy, who had lowered his head and looked embarrassed by Julia's assessment.

"Well, I'm glad you came here," she said. Julia looked up at her. "The children are safe in our spare beds. You are welcome to use one of the beds we have, as well. I'm sure I can find a cot to sleep on. We do all need to get some rest. Maybe we will be able to think more clearly in the morning and can figure out how Becky was involved with this necklace and the men who want it so badly. A good night's sleep is what we all need."

She had to admit it didn't look like anyone else agreed with her. But they all began to move slowly anyway.

Josie wasn't used to people doing what she told them or even following her suggestions. She hadn't really been the kind of girl to give many suggestions, much less orders. Adelaide directed Julia out of the dining area, whispering quiet reassurances.

15

Sleep had not come easy to Taylor that night. The result was a tired feeling the next morning when he rose. Josie had let him stay in her room while she bunked with her sister Belinda. He sat on her bed before going out to meet everyone else for breakfast, looking around, thinking about how Josie spent her time in that room. This was where she relaxed, where she slept, most likely where she prayed and pondered the wonders of life.

He sighed, pushing off the bed and heading out the door, taking a quick glance at himself in the mirror of her dressing table before leaving.

Coffee and bacon met his nose, and he breathed it in. The scents made him hungry. He delighted in the sounds of his children coming from the dining area.

He knew as soon as he stepped into the room that there were far too many people in there. The sisters, his mother, Larson, the children all moving around each other, talking, drinking, eating...

Taylor didn't mind it a bit. He moved into the action, crossing the room to the table, unnoticed until his daughter looked up from the children's sketchbook in her hands. Her eyes grew wide, and her face lit up with delight.

"Papa," she exclaimed. It was the same reaction she had every time she saw him, even if they'd only been apart a short time.

He held out his hands and waited for her as she bolted across the room and threw her arms around his waist. She was tall for five years, so he didn't pick her up anymore. It was awkward, and he was afraid he would hurt her. He dropped to one knee and hugged her.

"Good morning, darling girl," he said lovingly, looking into her happy eyes. "Did you get some good sleep?"

"I tried, Papa," the girl said earnestly, her face turning serious, her eyebrows pulling together, "but I was up very late. You were up very late, too, Papa."

Taylor nodded. "I sure was. And I didn't really get good sleep, myself."

Bella tilted her head, gazing at him sympathetically. "I'm sorry, Papa," she gushed. She threw her arms around his neck and gave him a tight squeeze that filled his heart with love and made him laugh.

"I'll be all right, darling," he replied, getting to his feet again. He crossed to the table, and Bella returned to where she'd been sitting between her grandmother and her brother.

Taylor went to Josie and sat in the open chair beside her.

When she looked at him, he wondered what the chances were that she was thinking about him the way he was thinking about her. If she was, would she ever say anything to him about it? Should he just come out and tell her how much he admired her and wanted to get to know her better? After seeing her with his children the night before, he knew it was only a matter of time before he just blurted it out. That was the kind of thing he did. He wasn't much for bottling things up.

His mother distracted him from his thoughts when she spoke, and he averted his eyes from Josie's face.

"I thought about it all night, Taylor," she said. "I

remembered some things that happened that would have tied this together for me if I'd been thinking about it. But now it seems like everything that's been strange has made sense."

"What are you talking about, Mother?" Taylor asked, keeping his voice gentle, as he always did with her.

"Becky. The necklace. I remember seeing a note from Becky, half-written. I didn't really read it. I simply scanned it out of curiosity. I wasn't trying to pry into her business. It was only because I was curious."

Taylor nodded, reaching out to softly pat his mother's arm. She looked so guilty. If only she'd really read the letter and had been the nosy busybody she was trying to avoid being. She might have already known what was going on if she had.

"It's all right, Mama," he murmured, "go on."

"It was a letter to her brother, Kenny. She mentioned the copy. The copy was ready, and she was bringing it to him in Oklahoma." His mother looked like she was about to break down. She probably felt like Becky's death was her fault for not putting the puzzle pieces together in time.

"Mother," he said, sitting forward, "what could you have done if you'd figured all this out before?

You couldn't have saved her. You wouldn't have been able to predict what happened. Just tell us what you know and stop feeling guilty. You are not to blame for anything. Anything at all."

His mother's appreciative look made him feel warm inside. "The letter said something about a family heirloom. I didn't even think about the copy of the necklace she'd had made when I read the letter."

"So you're saying the letter mentioned she was taking the copy to Oklahoma to Kenny, her brother," Adelaide said in a sharp tone.

Julia looked at the oldest Salinger sister and nodded vigorously. "Yes, that's right. Her brother, Kenny Dawson. I've been corresponding with him since her death. I haven't heard from him for several months. I thought nothing of that, though. I'm not his blood relative. He has no obligation to keep in contact with me."

Taylor's thoughts raced through his mind.

"How long has it been since you heard from him, Mama?" he asked. "Do you remember exactly? Or a close guess?"

She looked up into the air for a moment or two and then replied, "Three months come next Tuesday."

Taylor shared a glance with Josie. Before he could say it, she spoke up. "You said you first got a threatening letter here in Sacramento three months ago."

"That's just what I was thinking," Taylor responded.

"What does that mean?" Julia asked. Taylor looked at his mother.

"It doesn't really prove anything. But it does seem to suggest that Kenny let them know where we live. It also suggests that he's the one sending the letters and is after the necklace. He must have these men working for him, doing his dirty work."

Julia looked skeptical, which made Taylor curious. She didn't say anything outright, so he asked her, "You look like you don't think that's possible."

She was hesitant but finally answered him. "I've been talking to him, as I said, through letters for some time now. Two years. He first wrote to me after she... after we lost Becky. I expressed my sympathy, and we became friends. I don't think he's behind this. He's in a bad way. He told me he has... some problems. Gambling and the like. There are people he owes who are hunting him down. It just does not seem to me like he's the one doing the hunting. He always sounded scared in his letters."

"Did you hold onto any of those letters?" Josie asked.

Taylor didn't know if she was thinking the same thing as he was, but he was holding out hope the letters had a return address on them. He would compare the handwriting to the threatening letters, also.

"Why didn't you tell me about this before, Mama?" Taylor asked.

"He asked me not to," she replied, looking sheepish. "I didn't feel it was lying. He said you weren't even aware of his existence and that he wanted to keep it that way."

"I knew of him," Taylor grumbled, feeling resentful. Why wouldn't he know about his own wife's brother? He'd just never spoken to him, that was all. Becky had warned against it, saying Kenny was always up to no good and to let her deal with him.

If only he'd known that letting her deal with her brother would get her killed.

16

───────

Two days had passed since the revelation that Taylor's wife's death was indeed connected to the threatening letters and the necklace. Julia had retrieved the letters, but they didn't have a return address on them for Kenny. Only his name and the state of Oklahoma, followed by USA.

Josie thought it was a strange way to address an envelope. When asked how she got letters to him, Julia said she sent them to the postmaster's office in Kalamazoo, Oklahoma. He apparently got them because he mentioned them when he wrote her back.

Immediately following the discovery that the necklace was the object of attention, Taylor sent for it to be delivered to the bank vault there in Sacramento at the branch of his choosing. It was a relief when they heard back that the necklace was being brought by a courier.

Josie was in the big office with Adelaide, Larson, and Taylor when a knock at the door got their attention. Taylor looked at his pocket watch, standing up.

"That's got to be it."

Josie gave him a look of surprise. "You had it sent here?" she asked. "Shouldn't we go to the bank and make sure it stays completely secure?"

Taylor's smile was mischievous and made her feel tingly inside. "I told them it was a fake."

She wasn't sure how much reassurance that fact gave Taylor, but it didn't mean a lot to her. Fakes were just as easily passed off and killed over.

Was this brother the kind of man who would kill his sister for bringing him fake jewels to pay his very real debts?

Josie supposed it could happen. She didn't want to think that it could. But it could and probably did happen sometimes.

Taylor left the room and came back a few minutes later holding a long velvety jewelry box in one hand. He had a triumphant look on his face. He set the box on the desk in front of Adelaide and opened it.

Josie had seen necklaces before in her life. It wasn't like she wasn't privy to fancy jewelry or didn't have the money to purchase her own lovely pieces.

But there was something about that necklace that filled Josie with awe. It was a draping gold chain necklace with a deep green emerald placed in an arched gold frame in the shape of the gem, which was oval. Below the gem were three long loops of weaved gold chains. The entire necklace seemed to shimmer with life from the top clasp to the bottom of the golden loops.

Josie could tell she wasn't the only one overcome by the amazing beauty of the necklace. Adelaide and Sadie both had the same reaction, gasping and leaning over the box. They all touched the necklace softly as if pressing too hard would somehow damage it.

"What an incredible piece," Josie breathed. She heard her sisters agreeing with her under their breath.

"You realize we can't just hand this over to them," Adelaide stated in a firm voice. She had pulled away from the necklace, so Josie reached over and lifted the box up, bringing it closer to herself. The image of the princess wearing the jewelry passed through her mind, and she put color in where the camera had not. It was a stunning picture of magnificent loveliness.

Taylor came over and took the box from her hands without saying anything. She watched in stunned silence as he set the box back on the desk and removed the necklace from inside it. He moved so that he was behind her, and she instinctively lifted her hair from her shoulders. Her skin tingled with anticipation. She couldn't believe he was putting the necklace of a princess around her neck.

The eyes of her sisters were as wide as her own when the necklace came to rest on her chest. It was heavier than she'd thought it would be. When he moved his hands away, she knew he'd secured it behind her neck, so she lowered her arms, letting her dark hair rest on her shoulders.

"Take a look in the mirror," Taylor suggested casually as if he hadn't just brought Josie to her knees. "It looks beautiful on you."

Josie got up and moved to the large, framed mirror hanging by the door to the office. She was astounded to see the incredible necklace around her neck. It was much too fancy for the simple dress she was wearing, though she had picked something nice that morning, aware that Taylor would be there all day.

She touched it, murmuring, "I think it's the other way around. I look beautiful because I'm wearing it."

"No, that can't be it," Taylor responded immediately, "You don't need the necklace to be beautiful."

Josie's eyes snapped to his reflection in the mirror. He moved his eyes around the room, noticing that everyone was suddenly looking at him. His cheeks flushed when he realized he had given Josie a great compliment.

"Well, I... I won't take it back. It isn't a lie."

Josie turned from the mirror and crossed back to where she'd been sitting. She wanted to spare him any further embarrassment. "You are so sweet for letting me wear this. But you better take it off before I start believing I am a princess and ordering all of you to do my bidding."

She swept a smile over everyone in the room and was gratified when they all smiled back.

She turned her back to Taylor so he could unclasp the necklace and remove it from her neck. She lifted her hair to give him access to it and let her eyes settle on Adelaide, whose lips were twitching in a secretive way. It didn't take a close relationship with her to know what she was thinking at that moment.

Josie was thinking the same thing. She wouldn't mind it if Taylor started putting on all her necklaces. And everything else a beau would typically do for a woman.

When Taylor swept the necklace away from her, and the weight was lifted off, Josie immediately missed it. She watched him place it back in its box and cover it with the lid.

"You're very welcome."

"What's the plan, Adelaide?" Taylor asked, turning his eyes to the oldest sister. "Josie tells me you're the one to ask. What are we going to do now that we have the necklace? I'm not going to just hand it over because they tell me to. But having it is a good bargaining chip. Especially if they manage to get their hands on any of us and want to propose a trade."

"I'm really hoping that doesn't happen," Josie murmured, her eyes on the necklace once more.

"Me too," Taylor responded, giving her a direct look before moving his eyes back to Adelaide. "Newspaper ad?"

Adelaide nodded. "Yes. But we'll have to devise a plan that will catch them in a way where they cannot escape justice. They must go to prison. If they killed the two women. We need a confession. We need proof they did it."

"How are we going to get that?" Belinda asked. "Only a fool would confess to something unless there was enough evidence to convict in the first place, making the confession unnecessary."

"Some fools like to brag about their crimes," Josie said, an idea coming to her mind. She looked at Adelaide. "Perhaps I can be friends with these two men. Get them to talk to me."

Taylor grunted, shaking his head. "No." He sounded almost angry. "You aren't doing that. You already put yourself in enough danger. I'm not going to allow that. Fooling a man might work for a time, but when the truth is discovered, and a man feels betrayed and stupid, he will lash out. You will get hurt. If you see them again, it will only be to deliver the necklace."

"But we're not going to just give it to them, are we?" Sadie asked. "You said you didn't want to do that."

Josie rested her eyes on Taylor's face as he spoke. He was certainly easy to look at.

"No," he answered her, "but they don't know that.

Let's take the weekend and come up with a plan before placing the ad."

Josie stared at Taylor when he turned to her and asked, "Would you like to have dinner with my family and me tomorrow night?"

She looked at her sisters, who all looked as surprised as she was by the abrupt question.

"I'd like that," she said with a nod. "Thank you."

17

The fire crackling in the hearth beat back some of the chill in the air. Taylor stared into the flames, his mind deep in the recesses of his memory. He could see Becky on the day of their wedding, her big smile contagious, her laughter spilling out of her every few minutes. He'd never seen a woman happier in his life before or since.

For two years, Taylor had courted Becky, and he'd done everything in his power to make her happy. She was easy to please, and her easy-going attitude was reflected in their daughter.

Thinking about his children filled Taylor with a warm feeling of love—a sensation that was unmatched by any other emotion Taylor felt.

If Becky had the necklace copied in order to trade it for her brother's debts, she was doing so out of the kindness of her heart. She wasn't being devious. She had nothing to hide from him or anyone else.

Taylor sighed. If she hadn't felt like she had to hide it, he would have known about it. It was disappointing to think that his dear late wife hadn't trusted him enough to tell him about her brother's problems.

Or perhaps she'd been too embarrassed. That was a feeling Taylor could relate to.

Still, if she'd told him, he could have helped. He *would* have helped. He would have given her brother money to pay his debts. They didn't have to kill for the necklace, which, according to his mother, Becky had specifically mentioned was a family heirloom.

He rested his head back and let his eyes roam across the ceiling. The light was dancing in shadows here and there, making strange twisting shapes above him. He rolled his head to the side and let his eyes settle on the necklace, which sat in its open box on the table by the chair Taylor was sitting in.

He lifted his head and reached over for the necklace, taking it between his fingers and marveling at the weight of it.

He held it up and turned it back and forth, so the light reflected off it in different ways, creating beams of light in his eyes and sparkles on the walls around him.

Had Becky lost her life for this necklace? If yes, why? What was so special about this particular necklace? It wasn't the most beautiful in the world. It wasn't the most expensive or the most genuine. It wasn't anything that special. There were hundreds of princesses that wore jewelry as expensive and as beautiful as this piece.

But this was the one the bandits wanted. Taylor was positive they had killed both Becky and Clara for it. He examined it closely in the firelight. It had no flaws that he could see. It wasn't nicked in any way, and the emerald was smooth as can be.

"Are you feeling all right, son?"

Taylor turned at the sound of his mother's voice. Julia came into the room and placed herself firmly in a chair near him. He could tell she had a purpose. It was written all over her face.

"I'm all right," he answered softly. "Why? Are you all right?"

His mother shook her head. "No," she replied. "I'm not all right. Something is very wrong, and I... oh, I just can't seem to put my finger on it. I feel like there's something I've missed. So much I had forgotten to tell you and finally remembered. But there is something else. And I just can't shake the idea that it could be so very beneficial to you and to the agency in figuring all this out."

Taylor gave her a soothing look, leaning forward to place the necklace gently back in the box. "What is it you always told me? The more you stress about something, the more difficult it will be to overcome. That's what you always said."

"I have said that. It is true," his mother said with a nod. "Perhaps I should take my own advice."

"I know how hard it is, though," Taylor went on, moving his eyes back to the fire, slumping down even further into the chair, his arms flopped over the sides in a casual way. "it's easy to blame oneself in situations like this. Looking back and discovering you knew something all along that might have helped or might have prevented something from happening. If I had paid more attention to Becky's family, maybe this wouldn't have happened. If I had gotten to know her brother, or he'd felt I was approachable enough to come to for a loan. I would have even put him to work. None of this had to happen. None of it."

"You didn't let me blame myself for any of this,"

his mother said in an anxious tone that made him look over at her, "I'm not going to let you blame yourself. I corresponded with Kenny. He never said anything to me about it at all. He mentioned that Becky was going to help him before she was killed, but he never said anything about the necklace or made any reference that would make me think of it. He never blamed you or me or anyone in our family for what happened."

"Did he appear guilty in his letters? At all?" Taylor frowned when she shook her head. How could Kenny not feel any guilt for what happened to his sister? Knowing what they knew now, that her death was directly linked to the necklace and the delivery of it to Oklahoma—to her brother—Taylor couldn't fathom that the young man felt no guilt whatsoever.

"Just because he didn't express it to me doesn't mean he didn't feel it," his mother interrupted his thoughts. He pondered that for a moment and concluded she was probably right.

Over time, though, Taylor's anger at his deceased wife's brother was growing. He was holding Kenny responsible for everything that had happened in the two years since Becky's murder. And for the murder itself.

Until he had a chance to speak to the man and ask him certain questions, he would hold that belief. Or if the truth proved to be something different.

"You did send a letter to him for me, didn't you?" Taylor asked, sliding his eyes to his mother. She nodded. "Thank you. What did you say?"

"I didn't say anything different than usual, though I did mention that I'd been missing his regular correspondence. It wasn't always regular, though. Sometimes he would go a month or two without writing. So I don't know if he will respond this time either."

"It's all right," Taylor said in a grateful tone. "Thank you for trying."

Taylor left his eyes on his mother's profile for a few extra moments. Her pale skin danced with color as the flames lifted high in the fireplace. She was staring at it, lost in thought, her arms folded around herself, holding her shawl in place.

"Are you cold?" he asked.

She moved her eyes to him. He could see her love for him and felt blessed.

"No, son," she said softly. "I'm fine. But isn't it bedtime soon? You didn't sleep well last night. You should try to rest tonight. I can warm some milk for you if you like."

Taylor let out a soft chuckle. He knew his mother was joking. He didn't like warm milk and never had. His mother had been his rock since Becky's death—for all his life, really. She was the one person in his life he knew he could count on. She loved him unconditionally, and he knew it.

"Thank you, but no. I don't care for warm milk, which you well know. I will go to bed but only because I am tired. Not because my mother told me to."

She laughed, pushing herself to her feet at the same time he stood up.

"Good night then, son."

"Good night, Mama."

18

It felt like a million butterflies had gotten loose in Josie's chest as she walked from the buggy to the front door of Taylor's house. She and her sisters had spent an entire day with the family cleaning up after the break-in. They discovered during that time that nothing had been taken. Nothing at all.

The sound of her sister's excited voices still lingered in her mind. They'd helped her get ready, all the way from bathing to fixing her hair to picking out the perfect dress. None of them could believe how easily he'd asked her to dinner as if he had no qualms or insecurities in the world.

Now she had arrived, and her evening was about to begin. Before grasping hold of the knocker, she took in a deep breath and held it for a moment. Letting it out slowly, she hit the knocker against the door three times.

Josie cringed from the loud sound of it. She glanced around her, but there were no neighbors close enough to have heard it or seen her. Trees flanked the house on the left and right, blocking it from the nearest neighbors, who were still not very close by.

Taylor pulled the door open and gave her a big smile. "Josie. You look lovely. Please come in." He stepped back, his voice enthusiastic as he complimented her. The bubbling in her chest intensified.

"Thank you so much," she spurted as she passed him by. She looked around when she stepped into the foyer as if she'd never been there before.

"Everyone is in the parlor," he said, gesturing. "Come this way."

Josie followed him, delighted by the sight of the children on the floor playing with an array of brightly colored marbles and jacks. His mother was seated in a chair near them, able to reach down and help when she was needed.

"Hello there, Miss Josie," she said, grinning wide. "Children, look who has come to dinner."

Both children looked up at her, and Josie gave them a smile. "Hello," she said.

"You look pretty," Bella exclaimed, scanning Josie from head to toe.

Josie lifted one hand to cover her mouth, her cheeks burning. "Thank you," she replied. She'd never heard such enthusiasm in a compliment before.

"You're welcome." Bella said the words with just as much punctuation as her first proclamation. She looked at her brother, who just smiled at Josie again before turning back to their game.

"They just bought some new marbles at the general store," Taylor explained, holding out one hand to the couch. "If you'd care to sit, I'll get you a drink. White wine all right?"

Josie raised her eyebrows. "Yes. That would be lovely. How did you know I prefer white wine?"

"I saw the glass on your table in the restaurant."

Taylor went to the bar on the other side of the room and poured a glass of wine from a bottle that appeared to have been chilling in an ice bucket. Josie was impressed with his observation skills. That was very handy as a professional private investigator. Not that Taylor was one. But it was an impressive skill, nonetheless.

Josie took the glass from him before she went to the couch to sit down. Her heart skipped a beat when he sat down right next to her, his own glass of wine in hand.

"Have you had an exciting day?" he asked before taking a sip of the wine.

"No, thank goodness," Josie replied honestly. She was a little taken aback when both Taylor and his mother laughed softly. She moved her eyes from one to the other. "I don't mean to sound... oh, I don't know, lazy? I prefer it when there is less happening. Less means more time to sit back and enjoy living."

"You don't think that can be a bit boring?" Taylor asked, looking interested.

"I'm sure at times it can be boring," Josie replied, "but if you know how to fill your time so that you are enjoying life but being active, it's not. I don't mean sitting around being lazy. Lazy was the wrong word. I apologize for using it. Think of it this way. When you aren't being pressed to get something done, and you have no worries or concerns that require your attention, you have time to *live*. Truly live. Do you see?"

The look on Taylor's face was hard for Josie to decipher. He still looked interested in what she had to say. But he had something else on his mind, too.

Josie felt a surge in her chest. He looked like he wanted to kiss her.

She immediately denied to herself that was what she'd seen. It couldn't have been.

Could it? He *did* ask her to dinner with his family, after all. He hadn't extended that invitation to her and her sisters, just to her.

It was hard for Josie to fathom a man like Taylor Jameson could be interested in her as a sweetheart. He seemed so high society, so classy. Josie could have all the money in the world and still not feel classy on a level that Taylor exuded. She felt common next to him.

But Taylor didn't treat her like she was common. Nor did he treat her like she was a high society woman. He was just normal.

"I think that's a very interesting way of looking at our circumstances in life," Julia said, bringing Josie's attention to her. She had lowered her book, a contemplative look on her face. "I, too, enjoy the quiet things in life. But I also have to deal with these two." She swept one foot toward the children, a look of pure love on her face when she glanced at them. Josie moved her eyes to the children just in time to see Bella turn her head and grin at her grandmother, the look of adoration the older woman displayed reflected perfectly in her five-year-old features. Josie was touched by the shared glance.

"I'm sure they keep you feeling young, don't they?" Josie asked, forcing herself to get the question out without her voice wobbling with emotion.

"They do." Julia nodded emphatically. "They absolutely do."

Josie looked toward the door when she heard the distinct sound of a bell being tinkled. She looked at Taylor and his mother, wondering if it was all in her mind or if they heard the sound, too.

"Do you hear a bell?" she asked. "I think I hear a bell."

"Ah." Taylor pushed up from the couch. When he stood, his children hopped to their feet, and Julia set aside her book, also standing up.

Because of this, Josie was on her feet a few seconds later, feeling like she'd been called to attention.

"That would be dinner," Taylor said by way of explanation. He gave Josie a friendly smile. "I hired a young woman to come and cook for us tonight so my mother and I could have a break."

"You cook?" Josie asked curiously.

"Oh yes." Taylor nodded. "Mama wouldn't have let me grow up without knowing how to feed myself.

If I wasn't so good at what I do, I might have been a chef. Isn't that right, Mama?"

"That's right, son," Julia called over her shoulder as she ushered the children through the door and across the foyer to the dining room.

Taylor must have caught the amused look on Josie's face because he leaned close to her and said, "They are hungry. They were complaining about it before you arrived. I let them have apple slices, but Mama said that wasn't enough, and she wanted more."

Josie slapped one hand over her mouth to close off the laughter that threatened to erupt from her lips. She lifted her eyebrows at him, and he laughed all the way to the dining room.

19

Taylor was proud of his decision to get Marcy Mays from the Eastside Restaurant to cook for them. She did an amazing job and even served their plates and drinks as if they were in a restaurant. He could tell Josie was impressed when she cleaned her entire plate.

When he suspected dinner was over, he said to her, "Mother is going to put the children to bed and will meet us in the parlor. I thought we'd play some cards unless you are tired and want to go home?"

A sliver of relief passed through him when she shook her head and said, "No, no. I would never eat and leave. That would be so rude of me. I think a few hearty games of cards is just what's in order right now."

"Wonderful." Taylor slid his chair back and stood up. "Do you enjoy Spades?"

"Yes." She grinned at him. "I'm actually quite good at Spades."

"Oh." Taylor turned a serious glance to his mother. "Perhaps another game then."

He was gratified when Josie let out a delighted laugh. They went together across the foyer to the parlor where they had been. The card table was set up near the window, ready to go.

"Would you like an after-dinner coffee?" he asked, pulling out a chair for her and helping her scoot it back in. "I can go back and get some. Or tea. Or hot cocoa. Anything at all."

Josie shook her head. "No, thank you. I wouldn't say no to another glass of wine, though. I'm very impressed with your taste."

Taylor smiled. "I think I can do that for you. And you're right. It is good wine." He went across the room to the bar hoping she wouldn't expect anything more from him about the wine. He had no idea what it was, where it had come from, or if it was special in any way. As far as he knew, his mother had purchased it, as she was the one who kept the bar stocked. The two had never been heavy drinkers, so it wasn't replenished often, though he was fairly certain she'd recently purchased the wine.

"I'm glad you're able to relax, Taylor, considering everything that's going on."

He poured the wine quickly and returned to the table, sitting opposite of her. "I'm not sure relaxed is how I would describe myself," he said. "I am always on guard. If you mean asking you to come to dinner tonight in the middle of this investigation, well, it was spontaneous, I admit. But you've been truly remarkable, and I want you to know how grateful I am. I was impressed with the way you handled yourself with my daughter, the way you've volunteered to meet with these men, and I think we make an excellent team. Don't you?"

She looked thoughtful, her eyes never straying from his. "I do. I feel like I've known you much longer than ten days or so. You have lovely children. And your mother is a wonderful woman. It's clear that she loves you and the little ones very much."

Taylor nodded, moving his eyes out the window. "We were very happy when Becky was alive." He returned his gaze to her and added quickly, "Not that we aren't happy now. It's been two years, and although we do miss her dearly, we have come to accept there is nothing that can be done to reverse the situation. Life must carry on. The earth does not stop spinning when someone we love perishes."

Josie ran her tongue over her lips before taking a sip of her wine. "I know it isn't the same," she said softly, dropping her violet eyes to gaze at the top of the card table, "but I felt that way when my mother passed. We sisters, we were all grown. She had given us wisdom through the years, and we knew that she had loved us all. She loved Papa, too, and he was kind to her, kind to us. I loved growing up in my family."

"Have you and your sisters always gotten along as well as you do?" Taylor asked.

"We really always have. After we lost Mother, we relied on Adelaide, and she really took charge. She was there for Papa in every way she could be as his daughter, and we never gave any of his lady friends a hassle when they came for dinner."

Taylor lifted his eyebrows, amused by the observation. "Did your father have many lady friends over for dinner?"

Josie scrunched her nose at him in a way that made him feel a rush of adrenaline. "No, of course not. But there were a few, and we never denied him a chance at happiness. After a few years, we all decided it was because we intimidated them. There were four of us hovering around protecting our father even when we didn't mean to be. So for a while, we tried not to be there when he said he had company." She giggled, but Taylor heard the sadness underneath it. He could see it in her eyes, as well. "We didn't find out until later that the women stopped coming to dinner because Papa would rather spend his time with his daughters than a new woman. He realized what we were doing, and instead of telling us he'd rather have us around, too, he just gave up on ever finding love again."

Her words pulled on Taylor's heartstrings. "How awful for him. So he died alone?"

Josie blinked at him, and he realized his mistake.

"I don't mean died alone. Of course, you and your sisters were there at his side."

"He was not alone," Josie confirmed in a stern voice. He felt foolish and wanted to get past his flub as quickly as possible. He glanced quickly at the door to the parlor. His mother was taking her time. Probably for the exact same reason the sisters had avoided being home when their father planned a dinner with a lady. She was giving him time to talk to Josie on his own.

"I apologize," he said. "I didn't mean for it to come out sounding like that."

His mother came through the door at that moment and went straight to the bar, where she poured herself a glass of wine.

"You had the right idea ordering this wine, Taylor," she said, lifting her glass to him. "I may have gone and picked it up, but they told me at the general store that you asked them to get some of the best and put it on hold for you."

Taylor glanced at Josie and could tell by the look on her face that she knew he'd done that on purpose. He smiled at her.

"I know nothing about wine," he confessed with a casual shrug. "I just knew that you liked it because that's what you ordered at the restaurant. I reckon they know what's good a lot better than I do."

"You reckon?" Josie repeated back to him with a mischievous grin.

He laughed. "I reckon. Come on over, Mama, and play some Spades with us. I have a feeling Josie is going to be the big winner tonight, so don't bet the house."

Josie laughed delightedly, turning in her chair and settling in straight. "I'll try to be easy on the two of you," she said in a menacing way.

By the end of the night, Taylor knew he was going to want to spend a lot more time with Josie

Salinger. She was exactly the kind of woman he adored. She looked nothing like Becky but had the same generous nature, a quick smile, and his children obviously adored her.

All the more reason for the case to be solved as quickly as possible. He would just have to make sure she wasn't putting herself in unnecessary danger by keeping a close eye on her as often as he was able.

20

---

osie let down her hair and shook her head back and forth. She moved her eyes to the door as she ran her fingers through the strands, separating them, massaging her scalp with her fingertips. A smile came to her lips when Adelaide poked her head through the door.

"Are you decent?" she asked.

"Come on in," Josie said. Her smile widened when Adelaide didn't simply come in and close the door. She entered, followed by Belinda and Sadie, who both looked terribly excited.

"You have to tell us about tonight," Belinda gushed, pushing her glasses up on her nose as she plopped on the edge of Josie's bed. "I bet you had a wonderful time."

Josie's insides were still tingling from the night she'd had. "I will never forget it, that's certain," she agreed, nodding at them, moving her eyes from one to the other as they gathered in front of her. She turned sideways in the chair of her dressing table and held onto the back with both hands. "His mother is actually quite entertaining. She tells jokes."

Adelaide raised her eyebrows. "What kind of jokes?"

"The kind that makes the children laugh, too," Josie said. "She is very loved by that little boy and girl. It was so nice."

"But you didn't go there to spend time with Julia Jameson," Sadie prompted earnestly. "What is he like? Is he charming and fun or a boring old dodderer?"

"Dodderer?" Belinda gave Sadie a questioning look, which Sadie returned.

"Oh, you know what I mean."

Belinda laughed, turning back to Josie. "Well? Is he a dodderer?"

Josie looked from one to the other, amused by their banter. "He's not, as a matter of fact," she responded. "He's very charming and funny, too. He seems to be a fairly active father. By that, I mean he takes out time to do activities with the children because he has to work, you know. He wants to be in their lives and let them know he's there for them."

"That's the right way to be," Adelaide said in an approving voice. She leaned against one of the posts of Josie's four-poster bed and crossed her arms in front of her chest. "That's the way Papa always was, too."

"He didn't have to worry about it with us," Belinda put in, her fondness for their father evident in her voice. "We always made sure *he* noticed *us*."

The four girls laughed. Josie was swept into a memory that for her lasted much longer than the ten seconds or so when a pause of silence fell over them. She clearly saw herself and her sisters with their father at a festival when she was about ten years old. It would be three years before they would lose him, and the thought of not having him there never crossed any of their minds. He was young, vibrant, healthy, and strong. He would live forever, as far as they were concerned.

They planned ahead to attack him every time he mentioned work or was approached by a businessman who wanted to discuss something "important," grab onto his clothes and make him dance with them, probably there would be some tickling, they hadn't really decided what they were going to do. All they knew was that he'd been working too hard, and the festival was a time for him to relax. They weren't going to let him tense up because of work-related stress.

And that's just what they'd done. Josie let out a laugh, catching the attention of her sisters.

"Do you remember when we decided to attack Papa at that festival back when we were little?" She gave Adelaide a grin. "Well, you weren't little. I reckon you must have been about sixteen or seventeen then."

"I was turning seventeen that year. But I do remember that." Adelaide's voice reverberated with emotion. "We ended up attacking him a lot more than I thought we would. It seemed like that's all anyone wanted from him. Just business, all the time. It got to a point when I didn't think about him not being there. He was at work, and I knew it. I knew I would see him that night." Her voice broke with the last few words, and she stopped talking. Her face had turned a rosy red color, and she looked away from Josie with tears in her eyes.

Josie had lit a fire in her hearth in her room. All four of her sisters enjoyed cooler weather than she did, so she always had it blazing when they came in.

Generally, they stayed on the other side of the room.

So Josie was surprised when Adelaide pushed off the poster for the bed and walked to the fire, where she stood motionless, staring down at the flames licking the stones inside the chimney.

Belinda went after her, putting one hand on her shoulder. Josie understood why Adelaide still felt such strong sorrow after eight years. It still hit her sometimes that she would never see her father again. But she felt she was blessed by God with a gift. She was able to accept his death, and though she would always be mournful about it, she was certain he was in Heaven and better off than they were on earth anyway.

"Don't be sad," Sadie said, loud enough for Adelaide to hear and speaking in her older sister's direction. "We came in here to celebrate what might turn out to be a new love for our sister. Let's not get sad. That's not what Papa would want anyway. I want you to know something, Josie." She turned her eyes back to Josie, and a warm smile came to her lips. She leaned forward, her excitement returned to her face. "I am very happy for you. I approve of this match if one is made. Did he say anything about the future? I mean, will you be visiting his home again?"

"I'm sure I will," Josie replied with a grin. "I'm trying to find out who's sending these letters and who killed those women."

Sadie let out an exasperated gasp as she rolled her eyes, but her smile never left her face. "Honey, you know I mean something else. You know it. Stop teasing me."

Josie let out a pleased chortle. "Oh, all right. Yes. Yes, he mentioned that he would like to do it again. He said in a restaurant next time. Without his mother. He said he's too old for chaperones."

Her sisters laughed. She moved her eyes to Adelaide, who had turned back and taken a few steps closer, her face less sorrowful than it had been.

"I told him Adelaide might think I need one."

Adelaide laughed, shaking her head. "Now, now. Don't make him think I crack a whip."

"Oh, don't worry," Josie responded. "He knew I was joking. I told him I was."

"Thank you. What did you do? Did you have a good meal?" As she spoke, Adelaide came back to the bed, and the three sisters sat in a row on the edge, their eyes on Josie.

"It was so good," Josie gushed. "The food and the company. All of it. We played cards afterward. Their home is so nice when you look at it from that perspective and not one of a crime scene."

"Oh, I hadn't thought of it like that before," Belinda said. "It must have been very different."

"He is such an intelligent man," Josie said, lifting her eyes into her memory. "If he planned to talk about the necklace or the case, he didn't get his way. It wasn't mentioned all night. I learned a lot about him. A lot about his mother and his family and his past."

"And you want to see him again, don't you?" Belinda asked urgently.

Josie gave her a warm smile. "Of course I do. I wouldn't mind doing that for the rest of my life."

Sadie pulled in a deep breath, her mouth in the shape of an O. She opened her eyes wide, and she and Belinda began giggling excitedly.

Josie joined them, mostly because they were so excited about something that had nothing to do with them. It was sweet and touched Josie's heart.

21

Taylor stared down at the necklace. He'd been up most of the morning, only getting a few hours of sleep, his mind occupied.

It was important to him that Becky's killers were caught. But was it so important that he was willing to put the woman he now cared about at great risk? The thought came to his mind in the wee hours of the morning when he woke up with a start—completely wide awake—that even if he objected to their plan, Josie would go through with it anyway. It wasn't really up to him, even if he was the one paying them.

He'd drifted in and out of sleep until he finally got out of bed, removing the necklace and a pistol from the side table drawer and placing them on top while he pulled on his slippers and robe.

He took the necklace and the pistol downstairs to the kitchen, thinking if his mother was awake, she would jokingly offer him warm milk.

Taylor had just sat in one of the table chairs with a cup of hot cocoa he'd warmed on the stove when the door swung open, and his mother came through. He lifted the cup in her direction.

"There's more cocoa if you want some, Mother."

She nodded and crossed the room, taking a mug from the cupboard and pouring cocoa from the pot into it.

She sat opposite him, taking a sip. "You couldn't sleep either?"

"No. I did sleep, just restless. Not a long time. Lots of short naps."

Julia nodded. "That was me, as well. I worry about Josie. She is willing to go to great lengths to find Becky's killer. I suppose you know why she's so vested in it, don't you?"

Taylor looked down at his hands, which were folded in his lap. He was sitting back in his chair, his long legs stretched out to the side instead of under the table.

"I think I know, Mother," he mumbled, seeing

Josie's smile in his memory when he waved goodbye to her the evening after dinner.

"She's in love with you."

His eyes snapped to her face. "I don't know about that," he said hurriedly. "She may be attracted to me, but I wouldn't say she's in love with me. Not yet."

"I only say as I see," Julia responded, shrugging nonchalantly. "You have my blessing, of course. That is one smart girl with a good head on her shoulders. Besides, you have to marry her. She laughed at my jokes." She threw her head back and laughed herself, making Taylor smile.

"You're a card, Mama," he said jovially. "Already talking about marriage when I haven't known the woman more than a couple weeks."

"Sometimes, you just have to take a risk. You just have to believe that it's possible to have everything you ever wanted right in front of you. You deserve a good, loving woman, son. You had Becky, and she was taken from you. Now you have a second chance at happiness. I think you should take it."

Taylor raised his eyebrows, a playful smile on his face. "I asked her to my home for dinner," he said, "where my children and my mother live. We played cards afterward. What about my actions seems to tell you I'm not taking every chance I get with her?"

His mother giggled. "I'm glad to hear that. I suspected, but I just had to hear you say it."

"I guess you're just waiting for the chance to do your own thing again, are you?" Taylor was just teasing her, and she knew it. He continued, "Tired of those kids climbing up your legs morning, noon, and night."

She was shaking her head vigorously, a serious look on her face, and he had to laugh.

"No, no. Not at all. You know me. I don't want to go anywhere. I don't think Josie would be the kind of woman to demand that I leave or spend less time with the children."

Taylor also seriously doubted that. "I agree. She won't interfere with you or them."

His mother leaned forward and pushed the necklace, which was sitting in front of him next to the pistol. "Why do you have this out?"

"I was thinking about it. When I wasn't thinking about Josie and the future I'd like to have with her. I'm wondering if this is the fake or the real one. Are you sure Becky went through with having the fake one made?"

Julia looked thoughtful. "When she received the package with the fake one inside, she had the other one with it later. I saw it. I saw her putting them together, comparing them."

"So if this is the real one, where did the fake one go?"

"I'm assuming it was taken when she was killed," Julia responded. "I wish I'd thought of it sooner. It wouldn't have been on the list of reported stolen items because the real one was still safe and secure. You wouldn't have known it was missing."

Taylor's mind worked around the problem. He had figured out that Becky had been killed for the necklace, but the question had always been why. Now he thought he knew why.

"Do you think she promised them the real necklace, took the fake, and they killed her because they realized it was a fake?"

Taylor's eyes turned to his mother when she spoke. It was as if she had put his thoughts out loud into the universe. He blinked at her.

"I think so. It's the only thing that makes sense."

"But then why didn't they immediately come after you for the real thing?"

Taylor shook his head. There was still a lot he didn't know. So much he didn't understand. Still, he had a sense of satisfaction and felt they were making progress. He was meeting with Josie later in the morning—if he didn't go back to sleep—and they were set to place an ad in the paper requesting the meet with the bandits. If the sisters had come up with a plan for after, he didn't know about it. They hadn't contacted him on Sunday, and he hadn't attended church, preferring to take the day off to spend with his children. They'd had a picnic in the woods by the mountain at the end of the property and traipsed through the crunching leaves between bare trees, gray rocks, and shriveled bushes. He'd hoped for snow so the children could sled, but it hadn't happened.

"I'm going to talk to Josie this morning," he said. "If they killed my Becky because she had a fake necklace, I'm not going to let the sisters have another made for her to try to trade. That's not going to happen twice. Not for a necklace."

"Josie is very determined," Julia remarked, her voice low, her eyes on the piece of jewelry lying on the table. He couldn't tell whether she despised the piece or adored it. It had caused more trouble than it was worth. Plus, she felt guilty because she hadn't thought about the necklace when Becky died. He certainly didn't hold that against her. She would hold it against herself enough as it was.

"How much do you think it's worth?" he asked,

running his eyes over the emerald tucked away in its golden frame. "I never had it appraised. It was Becky who did that. That's why I don't know if this is the genuine article or not."

"I don't know how much it's worth," Julia replied, shaking her head. "She didn't tell me. I imagine it's quite a lot. That's the biggest emerald I've ever seen."

"Yeah, that's what I was thinking, too." Taylor leaned back more, letting the sun shine through the window behind him directly onto the gem. It flashed brilliantly.

He picked it up and scanned it closely, turning it from side to side, so the sun continued to reflect off it. It was beautiful. Unique. But it wasn't worth a human life.

And two had already been taken because of it.

22

J osie opened the front door and let Taylor in, hopping on one foot as she pulled on her shoe.

"I'll be... right there... hold on..." She hopped away from him, seeing the look of amusement on his face. She crossed the few feet to the mudroom and sat on the bench to finish tying her boot up.

"Is it very cold out there?" she asked. "It seemed cold when I opened the door, but sometimes the stoop is deceiving because it has a roof and the sun can't get all the way through to the door, so the space there can seem cooler than it would be if I'm..." She let her words trail off as she came out from the mudroom, looking up at him. The expression on her face made tingles explode in her body. "Why are you looking at me like that?"

His grin was so loving, she felt a little short of breath. "You are very... cute when you ramble on like that. It's cold out. You need your jacket. Your big jacket. You need your gloves and might want your earmuffs as well."

Josie spun around and hurried back to the mudroom, where she retrieved her heavy jacket, stripping off the light one she'd slipped on over her shoulders. His words had sent her heart into overdrive, but she was doing her best not to let him see it. He thought she was cute. *Cute.*

She bit down on her bottom lip, adrenaline pumping through her body. This could only be love. Nothing else felt like this.

She took in a deep calming breath, looked across the room at the wall, and told herself to relax. There was a case to solve. No telling what might happen before it's over.

Nothing that would put a wedge between them, she thought, turning around to go back to him.

THE WIND outside bit against her skin, making her wish she had a mask over her face. She pulled the large hat attached to her coat around her face to block it from slapping her silly.

"We'll be there soon," Taylor said, glancing at her. She returned his gaze.

"Is there going to be a blizzard?"

Taylor looked up at the sky, which was clear and blue. He moved his eyes back to her and shook his head. "I really don't think so. California isn't known for its blizzards. I've been in plenty back in New York, and this isn't the weather for it. I don't even know if they have blizzards here in California, do they?"

She gave him a blank look. "I don't know. I lived in Virginia for many years. There weren't many blizzards there, so I didn't get used to them."

"Then take my word for it. This isn't the right climate."

Josie was satisfied with that. She nodded.

She didn't come out from behind her big hood until she felt the wind die down. When she was able to put the hood down, she marveled at how pretty the land was without the green of leaves and grass.

"We should go for food after we put the ad in," Taylor said. "What do you think?"

"Yes, I'd like that very much," Josie replied, smiling. "Did you have a good breakfast, or is that why you're thinking about food already? You realize it will take us about fifteen minutes to put the ad in the paper, right?"

"I know. And no, I didn't have a good breakfast. No breakfast, as a matter of fact."

"Oh no. Why didn't you eat?" She gave him a concerned look.

He shook his head. "I was up last night thinking. Wondering about this necklace. Why anyone would kill over it. I never found out how much it was worth. That was Becky's thing. But I can't imagine it could be worth more than the price of a human life."

Josie understood where he was coming from. Nothing with a high monetary value was worth more than a human life. Nothing. That very evil had touched Taylor in a deeply personal way, and Josie's heart ached for him. She knew he wasn't the kind of man that sought pity or attention, but she considered it compassion when she rested her hand on his shoulder and squeezed.

"I know." She scooted a little closer in the wagon, so their arms were touching. "You are very strong for getting through after such a loss."

"I wasn't really given much choice," Taylor grumbled, his eyes fixed on the road ahead.

"Actually, you always have a choice," Josie heard herself saying. She'd heard these words from someone else, either her father or Adelaide. She couldn't remember which. Probably Adelaide. She was full of wisdom. "You can choose to go on after a loss, or you can choose to give up and waste away. People have been known to give up and waste away, never going anywhere in life. But you have more reasons than some to keep going, so I do understand how you feel. I just know that you actually do have a choice whether you want to go on living and thriving or go on living and suffering. Some people do. And it's so sad to see."

Taylor shook his head. "I can't do that. The girls need their father. They need me to be strong. Some might say they have their grandma, my mother, and yes, they do. But that's just more motivation for me to keep taking the next step forward." He gestured with one hand as if he was stepping forward with it. "Mother wouldn't give up on me. I sure won't give up on myself."

"You and your mother are very close, aren't you?" Josie knew they were. But she enjoyed hearing him talk about the older woman. He always had such nice things to say about her.

"Oh yes, she's my rock. I've said it before, and I'll say it again. I don't know where I would be if it wasn't for her. She's always been there for me."

"I love that. That's how I feel about my sisters. Sisters don't always get along. The four of us are just lucky, I guess."

"Blessed is more like it," Taylor remarked, moving his eyes to her face for a moment. He seemed to examine her features momentarily before looking back out over the road. "Luck had nothing to do with it. Before you four were born, God said he needed four good sisters, and there you were. He works in mysterious ways, you know."

Josie laughed. "I have heard, yes."

THEY PULLED up in front of the newspaper offices fifteen minutes later, and Josie got down without assistance. Taylor rounded the wagon but not in enough time to help her down. She looked at him sheepishly, wishing she'd waited. He looked bereft for a moment and then offered her his arm.

"Shall we go in?"

"Yes, sir, I think we will."

She took his arm, delighted for the chance to be linked with him so intimately, and the two walked through the door into the office.

The receptionist had a desk directly in front of the entryway, and right behind it, in an enormous room with glass on all four sides, was the biggest printing press Josie had ever seen. It was also shiny clean. She assumed it was new and thought for a piece of equipment, it was a fine-looking machine. She was amazed by it the first time she came into the office and was amazed by it this second time as well.

"We need to place another ad," Taylor said, plunking down a piece of scrap paper on which he'd written the message to the bandits. "This is it. Please let me know the cost."

Josie moved her small handbag around to the front and unclasped it, intending to get the money for the ad. Taylor put one large hand over hers to prevent her from taking out any money.

"I'm paying for this," he said.

"But it's an expense," she protested.

"Which means I'd end up paying it anyway by giving it to you in your fee. Please. I will pay. Put your money away. I have it."

23

A cold chill ran across Josie's arms and down her spine when she took the letter from the postman. His smile was big, and she returned it, but hers was less enthusiastic. She knew where the letter had come from. The ad had given the address of the agency for the bandits to contact instead of sending a letter to Taylor's home. She had promised to cooperate with them.

It had been three days since they placed the ad, the same amount of time it had been from the first contact with the bandits.

With shaking hands, she tore open the envelope and pulled out the folded paper. Before she could read it, though, a cold wind blasted across her face, lifting her dark hair and freezing her bare legs under her dress.

She hurried back inside, slamming the door shut against the bitter weather. She could hear her sisters talking in the main office and went in that direction, looking down at the letter and reading the words quickly. What was written there made her heart go into overdrive. She didn't know whether to be excited or worried. So she chose to be both.

Josie waved the letter frantically as she went into the room. "It's here," she hissed. "Their letter. It's here."

"What does it say?" Belinda asked breathlessly, leaning forward in her chair as her sisters were doing.

Josie read from the letter, which was brief and to the point. "It says I must go to the train station and pick up a ticket for a northbound ticket to Oklahoma." She looked up at her sisters. "I'm fair certain that Taylor's wife was on her way to California. It had something to do with her brother."

"Well, we already knew this had a connection to his sister."

"And the other woman," Josie said, resuming the seat she'd had earlier. "There's only one explanation I can think of that could be why she was killed along with Becky. I think the bandits, these outlaws, must have thought the other woman had the necklace. This whole thing is so they can get their hands on it."

"It's sad that something can be so valuable lives have to be taken for someone to possess it." Sadie shook her head, moving her eyes around to her sisters. She was arched back in her chair instead of sitting upright in it, her hands folded in her lap. "I wouldn't even have anywhere to wear it to. It's too fancy. We don't have balls with lords and ladies or anything like that."

"You should wear it when you get married to Taylor," Belinda said mischievously, winking at Josie.

"Oh," Josie cried out, her cheeks getting hot. She looked away, rolling her eyes.

"You think I'm joking, but I'm not. I can see the two of you together forever. Those children love you, and you're very good with them." The look of joy on her face changed, and she gave Josie a forlorn look. "Oh, but I'll miss you when you move to his big house. You'll have to come and stay sometimes." She looked at her other two sisters. "Oh, dear. I think I'll be the only one left here after you two are married and gone, too. The lonely spinster doing all the work behind the women of action."

Josie laughed softly. Her sisters immediately launched into encouraging words for Belinda, telling her that she wouldn't be a lonely spinster and her time would come. All she could think about was the idea of marrying Taylor. Belinda had said it out loud, but it wasn't like Josie hadn't been thinking about it, too. He had asked her to dinner, her specifically. Not her sisters and her. He wasn't asking the agency to come to dinner. He had asked her.

Their night had been wonderful, and even though they hadn't seen each other the day before, he'd stayed on her mind, and she hoped she'd been on his.

"Josie," Adelaide said her name and caught her attention. She looked up at her oldest sister. "You look like you're in a trance. Are you worried about this trip? We will have to make arrangements, you know. We will need to be on the train, too. I'll get Deputy Andrews. Fill him in on what's going. Larson will be there, of course." She looked at Sadie. "Where is that man of yours anyway?"

"He went to the horse auction."

Adelaide nodded. "Good. We need a new horse. When will he be back?"

"Probably this afternoon. The auction goes until four o'clock. I don't know if he'll stay that long. If he doesn't see anything he likes by two, he'll probably give up and come home. And if he does see something he likes, he'll get it and still come home."

"I see." She returned her gaze to Josie. "Why don't you go get Taylor? Tell him what's going on. And Julia. Make sure you tell her. She was fond of Becky, and I think she feels guilty about what happened to her since she was the only one who knew about the fake necklace. Tell him your theory about the other girl being killed because they thought she had it. All of this needs to be told to the lawmen in New York. The ones in charge of these cases."

"Taylor didn't seem to have much faith in them," Josie said, "but I agree. They do need to know. I think any arrests are going to be made here, though." She dropped her eyes to the letter in Adelaide's hand. "Probably on that train."

"We can't make an arrest on the train without the deputy," Sadie said, taking the letter from her sister and looking down at it. "I wonder why they want to do it like this? Becky was on a train when she was killed. They know we know that. They have to. Are they taunting us? Taunting Taylor?"

"The motive behind it all is still beyond me," Josie said, moving her eyes between the three women in front of her. She held out her hand. "But let me get this letter to Taylor. We'll go to the train station and get the ticket."

"It says to put an ad in the paper for tomorrow, letting them know you will be there," Adelaide said, handing her the letter. "So don't forget to do that when you pick up the ticket."

Josie nodded. "Don't worry, I won't forget."

24

———

Taylor saw her coming through his front window just as he was going to the door to check the weather. He was surprised by how good it felt to see her face. He was covered by a warm feeling of desire and opened the door wide, smiling. "Josie. How good to see you. Come in." He looked to the left and the right, quickly glancing to see the wind blasting through the trees that lined the sides of his home.

Josie hurried past him and shook herself as soon as she was inside.

He closed the door.

"Oh, you have it so warm in here," she exclaimed, turning her back to him.

He reached up and grasped the shoulders of her

coat, helping to ease it off her shoulders. He hung it on a hook in the mudroom near the door and set her earmuffs, gloves, and hat on the bench just below her coat.

"I do like to keep it as warm as I can," Taylor said, secretly hoping she didn't have an objection to that. He had a problem with having a constant chill and always being cold. He didn't like it and kept things warm whenever he could. "Summer is my favorite season. I don't care for the cold weather."

Josie's face brightened with joy. "I am the same way. I keep my bedroom much warmer than the rest of the house because my sisters don't like it. They don't put fires in their rooms nearly as often as I do. They rely on the main fire down in the parlor and the heat coming through the vents."

"That's not enough for you, I assume?"

She shook her head. He didn't mind it at all. In fact, it was perfect for him. They would get along fine on that issue.

"I got a letter from the outlaws," she said, pulling the folded paper from her handbag and handing it to him.

He opened it and read the words there. It was just what he'd thought. She was going to be put in harm's way, just like Becky. His first instinct was to shake his head and tell her it was impossible. She had already turned away from him and was heading for the parlor, so he followed her.

"Josie…" he said slowly. "I don't think this is a good idea. You'll be in the exact same position as Becky was. She was killed. I can't let that happen to you. I would never forgive myself. Your sisters would blame me. I wouldn't—"

"I'm going to do it, Taylor," Josie replied, just as he'd expected her to, "but you need to keep something in mind that should help ease your fears at least a little."

Taylor clamped his mouth shut, looking into her eyes. She'd turned around and stopped so that she was standing directly in front of him, only a few inches away. She was practically within kissing distance. Taylor didn't mind that. Not a bit.

"What do I need to remember?" he asked softly, resisting the urge to grab her.

"This time it's different. You know what's going on. You can help stop it."

"You think they will go through with it if I'm with you?"

"You won't be with me," Josie said, turning again and crossing the threshold into the parlor. She went to the bar and poured two glasses of white wine.

Taylor couldn't help feeling pleased by how comfortable Josie was with him and his home. It was as if she lived there too.

Maybe sometime in the future, she would.

"If I'm not with you, then how is it going to be different?"

"Because you know what's going on." She handed him one of the glasses and sat down on the couch. He lowered himself to sit next to her, facing her at an angle. "You didn't know last time. And I'll have a deputy with me, at least. I'm sure Adelaide will be on the train."

"I have to be on it, too," he insisted. "I want to be as close to you as I can get. I won't stay away. I can't let what happened to Becky happen to you."

He was surprised by how confident Josie looked. He wondered how she managed to be so calm and collected when it was her very life at stake. She didn't look like she thought the murderers were very dangerous.

"Aren't you worried about any of this?" he asked. "You don't look like you are."

Josie lifted her eyebrows, taking a sip of her wine. "I am about as nervous as a hen when the fox is around," she admitted softly, "but this is the job I signed up for, and you are... very important to me.

You and your children and your mother. I think about how awful it would have been for you if something had happened to them when those men raided your house. They could have been..." She lowered her voice, "killed."

"My mother is too quick-witted for that," Taylor said, pride for his mother filling his heart, making him puff out his chest.

"Yes. She's an amazing woman. Adelaide told me you and I should go get the ticket and place the ad for tomorrow's paper telling them I'll be on the train. And I suppose I'll need to pack a bag. You can come back to the house for that. Unless you have business to attend to."

Taylor shook his head. "No, I cleared everything up for today. The branch I opened here can manage without me until we get this sorted out. I don't do anything but supervise anyway. Plus, I have some incredible supervisors that take care of the crews."

Josie smiled over at him, her violet eyes sparkling. He felt a surge pass through him but resisted the strong urge he had to lean forward and kiss her.

"I'll bet you are a good boss to work for," she said. "Your employees love you, don't they?"

Taylor thought about that for a moment. He

didn't particularly know many of his employees. He had managers to take care of that. He knew only the men directly under him in seniority. They did everything from that point on.

"I suppose I don't really know any of them," he confessed. "They seem to be happy. I don't lose employees, there are no accidents, and everyone seems to get along, both the men here and the ones in New York. That is a blessing for me, I promise you. I don't have much to worry about when it comes to business." He noticed her glass was getting low. "Would you like to ride out to the train station now, or would you prefer another glass of wine?"

Josie looked down at the glass. She grinned at him, turned the glass up, and drank the rest of the liquid inside. She let out a satisfied "ahh" afterward and set the glass on the coffee table in front of the couch. "That letter got to me a little more than I thought it did," she said. "I just needed to calm my nerves."

Taylor had to chuckle. Here he was thinking she was completely calm when in reality, she was hiding the fact that she was a bundle of nerves.

"In that case, let's go, my dear." He stood up and held on hand out to her. "We'll take my buggy. It's ready to go, as I expected I'd be coming to you shortly."

Josie took his hand and pulled herself to her feet. He loved the gentle touch she had and how soft her skin was. He didn't want to let go, though he knew he had to.

To his surprise and pleasure, she didn't let go right away. She allowed him to hold her hand until they got to the front door.

"Oh," she grunted, "I have to get all that back on again."

He laughed. "Don't worry, I'll help you. It doesn't really take that long."

"No, it doesn't," she admitted, "but sometimes I like to grumble about it."

Taylor's heart jumped in his chest. He touched her dark hair and brushed it back from her face. "It's okay. You're cute enough to get away with it."

25

Josie rode beside Taylor, shielding her face from the cold by pulling the hood of her coat around her head and leaving only her nose, mouth, and eyes in the open. It was only going to get colder. She was glad the case was wrapping up.

They had placed the ad in the paper and picked up the train ticket afterward. As they were leaving, Josie spotted the two men loitering outside the station. She pretended like she hadn't seen them, grabbing Taylor's arm and holding him close to her.

He looked down at her in surprise. "Are you all right?" he asked.

"I see them," she hissed, turning her eyes in the direction the men had been. For all she knew, they'd already retreated into the woods, and when he looked, he wouldn't see them. Then he would think she was losing her mind.

"Yeah, they're over there," he confirmed a second later. "Don't you worry. They wouldn't have set up this elaborate scheme if they were going to jump us now. They don't know if we have the necklace on us. In fact, they probably know we don't. How stupid would it be to carry that around on a regular basis?"

"It would be very stupid," Josie answered him.

They reached the buggy, and as Josie pulled herself up onto the bench seat, she slid her eyes casually in the direction of the outlaws.

They were still there, just standing idly, watching her and Taylor leave the train station. One of them was smoking a cigarette, as indicated by the curling smoke that rose from his fingertips and the clouds that came from his mouth that were thicker than the typical cold air steam clouds.

"Let's get out of here," she murmured, moving as close to Taylor as she could get as they left the lot. He didn't seem to mind. She moved even closer.

"You must be really cold."

Josie was cold. She would admit to that. But the real emotion she felt at that moment was fear. Taylor was right. She was putting herself in the same position as Becky had been. They had strangled her, but they'd shot Clara. To her, that meant they were willing to do whatever they had to.

Thinking about Clara brought her and her sisters' conversation into mind.

"The girls and I were thinking about the necklace and the connection to the murders. We thought Becky was killed because she had a fake one instead of the real one."

Taylor nodded, his face showing his agreement, as well.

"And we think Clara was killed because they thought Becky had given her the real one."

"How would they even know who Clara is?" Taylor asked incredulously, disgust lacing his words. "She was a completely innocent victim in this, not that Becky wasn't. But she was more so than Becky."

"Yes, it's awful," Josie added, shaking her head. "Poor girl didn't do anything at all. And to have her life snuffed out that way. Just awful."

"I think your theory is right."

"Adelaide said you should tell the lawmen in New York, but I think the men they are seeking are here. She's talking to her deputy friend right now and telling him everything that's been going on. He'll be the one on the train with me." Her voice caught in her throat. She glanced over at him, knowing she'd just revealed how nervous she really was.

Taylor's eyes moved to examine her face. He lifted one arm and wrapped it around her shoulders, pulling her as close to him as he could. "I want you to know how brave I think you are for doing this, Josie. You don't have to. I can still meet them."

"They will kill you if you meet them."

"They might kill you," Taylor retorted sharply.

She shook her head. "They aren't going to kill me. They might try, but they won't succeed. The deputy will be there. I will be safe. And even if I have to give them the necklace, they will never get off the train with it. There will be law enforcement at the station when we get to the next stop. They will board and arrest the two men. That was the arrangement Adelaide said she was going to make anyway."

Taylor looked thoughtful. "I have to admit that is a good plan. Maybe you should just hand it to them, no questions asked."

Josie shook her head, rejecting that idea. "No, I want to see how much information I can get out of them. I want to know if they feel any regret at all for killing two innocent women over a piece of jewelry."

Taylor's lips twitched. "They aren't going to tell you they regret it," he remarked, "even if they do."

Josie knew he was right. But she was an observant woman. It came naturally because she was shy on a normal basis and spent most of her time watching how others (like her two older, more vibrant sisters, Adelaide and Sadie) behaved and choosing what she could and could not mimic. Over the years, she'd grown into her own person, choosing to do things on her own instead of copying someone else. But she'd never lost her observational skills.

"I believe I will be able to tell," she replied. "I think I can sense when someone feels a certain way. I can read it on their faces. It's not so much the words as it is the way they look at me and at things around them. The words, too, but people lie with words. They don't lie with their faces."

"Let's go to the cafe and have a nice hot cup of coffee."

"Tea for me," Josie said, shivering, allowing her teeth to clack together. "Yes, let's hurry, please."

They got to the front of the cafe, and Josie jumped from the seat, jogging around to the back and grabbing a large horse blanket from the bed of the wagon. She quickly went back to the animals and threw the blanket over the back of the horse on the passenger side of the wagon. Taylor did the same for the other horse.

He came around the animals, grabbed her hand, and pulled her up the short steps quickly. The cold air bit against her cheeks as she went up, crossed the foyer, and waited a moment for him to open the door.

A blast of heat hit her in the face, and she smelled the wonderful scent of burning wood. She closed her eyes when she was inside, removing her coat with Taylor's help.

"Oh, it's so warm in here," she expressed, draping her coat over her arm and heading toward the huge stone fireplace to their left instead of going to a table and sitting. In front of the fireplace were three long couches, forming a U in front of the fire. She dropped her coat to one of them and went to the hearth, holding out her palms to the flames, absorbing as much heat as she could.

She sensed when Taylor came up beside her and glanced to see his profile was as handsome as ever.

"Tomorrow is an exciting day," Taylor murmured, glancing down at her. "I hope you will have dinner with us at my house tonight."

"I would love to have dinner," Josie replied, "but

you had better not be inviting me because you don't think I'll be coming back."

"What a morbid thought," Taylor said with a frown. "No, I wasn't thinking that."

"Good. In that case, I would love to have dinner with you and your family. I think I'll bring my sisters this time, though. You know, in case it really is a last supper."

"Good Lord." Taylor gave her an astonished look. "Don't say things like that, I beg of you."

Josie laughed. The fire had filled her with warmth, so she turned away. "Let's get a table near here," she said. "I don't want to be cold. I'd eat right here if they'd let me."

"They might let us sit on these couches. I've never asked before."

"Let's ask." Josie felt an exuberant amount of excitement for such a simple thing. She wanted to enjoy every moment she could get with Taylor. She couldn't allow herself to really think something might happen to her the next day. She couldn't really even think the words.

But that wasn't going to stop her. She wouldn't let her fear make her back out of doing what she needed to do. While it was true Adelaide could prob-ably make the meeting in her place, she was determined to show them all that she was as brave and bold as they were.

The café was buzzing with people, but none of them looked at Josie and Taylor. They were busy with their own lives and circumstances. Josie looked around at them, settling onto one of the couches while Taylor went to speak to the serving girl.

Sacramento was a bustling city. She didn't know everyone, only a small circle of people, in fact.. Those she did know were decent human beings, hard workers, things that made a person a success in America. It was hard to imagine anyone would be evil and wicked enough to end the life of a young woman, of two young women, because they wanted something worth a lot of money.

If Josie was brutally honest with herself, she was sickened and disgusted by the very thought and hoped the men responsible would meet a painful and untimely end.

26

Her heart slammed nervously in her chest. Her blood was running cold through her veins, like ice sliding through her from head to toe. The train was rolling up to the station, louder than anything Josie had ever heard before. She was fond of traveling on a train, despite the sound. In fact, she found the sounds a train made to be quite soothing, excluding the squeal of the brakes when pulled to the extreme.

Josie pulled in a deep breath and let it out slowly. Her sisters were there, but they were standing more toward the building. Taylor wasn't there, but Josie knew he would show up. Probably at the last minute. The only reason her sisters weren't standing with her was that they didn't know if the outlaws knew they were her sisters. She didn't want them in danger because of her. The outlaws might have followed her to her house or to Taylor's house, but she'd never caught sight of them.

"Last chance to get out of this," she murmured. There actually wasn't any last chance. She wasn't backing down or giving up. She might be working on her boldness and courage, but she wasn't about to turn tail and run.

The necklace felt like it was burning a hole in the small pocket she'd sewn into her favorite dress some years ago. She rested her hand to her side and pressed her palm against the bump, pushing it against her waist. It was there. It wasn't going anywhere.

Her heart jumped in her chest when she spotted Taylor coming onto the platform and heading in her direction. Her eyes darted all around her, looking for the bad men. She didn't see them but didn't want to take any chances. What if he came over to her and they saw him and then decided to shoot him dead from a distance?

Her panicky thoughts raced through her mind. She hurried in his direction and gestured with her head that he should go toward the building. There was a small alcove between two large metal lockers apparently used for storage or some such use. She slipped in between them, where there was just enough room for four people to hold a conversation without being right on top of each other.

"I wasn't going to not come and see you off, Josie," he said somewhat breathlessly. The look of anxiety on his face touched Josie's heart.

"Don't worry about me," Josie said, placing one small hand on his arm. "Look." She moved her eyes to the deputy, who was waiting for the train, looking like he had no cares in the world.

"What if they see him get on?" Taylor asked. "They will know he's there to get them."

"He's not going to pay them any attention at all," Josie replied. "He knows what they look like based on the sketches Adelaide made, but he isn't going to do anything until the right time. I promise."

"How will he know when the right time is?" Taylor sounded reluctant. "I should really be the one doing this."

Josie scowled, though her heart was filled with love for the man. "Stop it, Taylor. You have children to consider. They can't be without their papa."

"And your sisters can't be without you," he replied in a determined voice. "Let's just call it off. If I see them, I'll simply throw the necklace at them and get you out of here. In fact, give it to me, and I'll do just that."

Josie was overwhelmed by his fear for her. She'd never had anyone so protective, anyone that made her feel completely secure at all times.

"Taylor," she whispered slowly, "I have to do this. You know I do. It's the only way. I'm going to get them to confess to murdering those women. I promise you. I'm going to do my best."

"If anything happens to you, I don't know what I'll do with myself."

He looked so aggravated. Josie wanted to comfort him, but the situation was unlike anything she'd ever experienced before. She tried to put herself in his shoes, remembering that he'd lost his wife this way. That for two years, he hadn't known what really happened, and he was just about to get his answers.

No wonder he was on edge. Who wouldn't be?

The train pulled to a stop, and they watched as the deputy got on.

"They have to board here, too, don't they?" Josie asked, moving her eyes up and down the platform. She didn't see them. "What if they don't get on? Then what?"

"Then you stop at the next station, get off and

come back. You didn't pay for this ticket, but you can pay for one to come home, can't you?"

"I would have had to anyway," Josie replied with a nod. "I just don't know why they would miss the train when they know I'm getting on it."

"Maybe they are staying behind until they see you board," Taylor added, wonderment in his voice as he moved his eyes around. "I don't see them either."

It was now or never. Josie knew she had to get on that train. She had no idea how long it would stay there at the station.

She looked at Taylor longingly, wishing he would kiss her good luck.

When their eyes met, she felt a surge through her body that left her feeling a bit weak. She was fully aware of how hard her heart was pounding.

Josie was only seconds away from turning toward the train and leaving him behind when he took both her upper arms in his hands and pulled her close. She tried to control her breathing as he drew her nearer until his lips were pressed against hers. It felt like her heart exploded in her chest.

When he let her go, she was breathless, staring into his eyes with as much desire as she saw in his.

"Come back to me safe," he whispered. "You hear?"

She nodded and, without another word, drifted away from him, glancing back several times as she made her way across the platform and to the door where an attendant was waiting. He stepped to the side, and she went up and into the car.

The kiss lingered on her mind as she moved down to a compartment that was empty. She went in and closed the door behind her, drawing the curtain. She went to the window and bent at the waist, placing her hands on the sill, peering out. She could see her sisters. They were looking at the windows, searching for her. She scanned to her left to the spot between the two enormous storage lockers.

Taylor was no longer there.

She didn't see the two men boarding either. But they might already be on the train for all she knew. Sacramento was a busy city, and they weren't the only ones taking the train that day. They could easily have blended into the crowd.

Josie's eyes swayed back to her sisters. They had spotted her and were waving frantically. Adelaide threw her a kiss. She had been surprised that morning when Adelaide said she wouldn't be on the train. The only one there to protect her would be the deputy and anyone he brought with him. He'd been standing by himself on the platform, so she suspected he hadn't thought to hire anyone else. Or maybe he just didn't want to look suspicious, causing the outlaws to run.

She waved to her sisters, giving them the most confident smile she could muster. Adelaide threw her a kiss, and she returned it.

Josie sat down on one of the bench seats, placing her handbag in her lap. How long would this trip take? What was going to happen?

The anticipation and apprehension were nearly overwhelming. Josie willed herself to calm down. She would be safe. She would question the men and see what she could get out of them, but if it came down to it, she would take the smart route and just give them the necklace. It was risky, but they would be taken into custody the next time the train stopped anyway.

If everything worked according to plan.

27

As soon as Josie's back was turned, Taylor left the area between the storage lockers, glancing quickly to see if Adelaide and the other sisters were watching him. They weren't. Their eyes were glued to their sister as Josie got on the train. Taylor moved across the platform to the end and hopped off the edge, jogging quickly to an outhouse next to the side of the building.

He went inside and bent down to dig into the dirt in the right-hand corner. Just under the surface of the dirt, he touched the top of a fabric bag. He pulled the bag out and dumped it on the ground.

He had no real idea how to attach the wig to his head. He'd taken the recommendation of the lady in the wig shop which one to buy and had gotten a brief explanation from her, but he didn't have time to apply the wig properly. The train could leave at any minute.

He picked up the pair of oval eyeglasses he'd purchased and put them on. The wig went on his head next. Last but not least, his hands shook slightly as he applied a small amount of glue from a tube he dumped out of the bag to the back of a false mustache. He pressed it against his upper lip until it felt secure, and he could twist his lip back and forth without it falling or sliding off. It didn't need to stay on long. He just needed to get on the train without being seen.

He smoothed the wig down over his hair, making sure it was all tucked up inside before placing his hat back on his head. He'd stuffed a new shirt and vest in the bag and pondered only for a second if he should bother with that. Who had noticed what he was wearing before?

He didn't take long to decide. He heard one of the attendants calling out and heard the whistle of the train. It would depart soon.

He decided at the last minute to wear the same shirt but to change vests, as one was darker than the other. He didn't want to take any chances.

He buried the sack in the same hole, kicking dirt

over it until it was hidden. It was in a dark corner anyway. Someone would have to be looking for it and know it's there to find it.

Taylor left the outhouse behind, hurrying to the platform and hopping up on it. He went to the first train entryway he approached and hopped up into the train. He wanted to look over his shoulder to see if the sisters had seen him, but he was afraid to give himself away, so he continued into the train, heading in the direction of the car Josie had boarded.

Taylor passed from one train car to the next until he was in the one he knew Josie had boarded. He walked along the corridor, glancing quickly in through the windows of the compartment doors. Three of the windows had pulled drapes. Disappointed, he thought quickly about what to do.

When he passed a compartment that was empty, he slipped inside and closed the door behind him. The train was about ready to leave, so he felt comfortable he could hide in there until the time was right. He didn't have a plan yet. All he'd prepared for was to get on the train. He'd decided to take it moment by moment once he was on the train.

He decided then and there that his plan was stupid and he should have been more careful with details. Now he was stuck on a train about to move with no plan on how to rescue Josie and escape the outlaws.

He bent down and peered through the small window. He moved his eyes to the left and then to the right.

"Where are you, Josie?" he murmured.

At that moment, the compartment door across from him and two down opened. His eyes widened, and he jerked sharply away from the window when he saw Josie's head pop out. Fortunately, she was looking away from him first. He was out of her sight before she turned her face toward him.

Taylor couldn't help the huge smile that came to his face. He looked up at the ceiling, sending a prayer of thanks to God. "That was really helpful," he mumbled.

He heard the door of the compartment close but stayed back for another minute, thinking she might be outside the compartment, watching for whoever was coming for her.

A second later, he heard her whispering voice. Tingles spread over his skin. It took a moment for him to realize she wasn't talking to him.

"Are you there? It's me. Are you there?"

A responding male voice came back and answered her. Taylor realized he was listening to the deputy, who must have been in a compartment next to Josie.

"I'm going to keep the drapes closed to the window on my door," Josie whispered sharply.

Taylor wanted badly to look through the window, but it sounded like she was right outside his door. If anyone else in the car heard her, they would probably be very curious.

"I'll be watching. Don't you worry."

Josie didn't respond to the deputy. Taylor listened but could hear nothing. Seconds later, the sound of a door closing met his ears, and he realized she'd gone back to her compartment. She'd only been checking—reassuring herself that help was very nearby.

He was grateful that the deputy sounded so confident when he answered Josie. He hoped it made her feel secure, too.

The one thing Taylor worried about most was that the outlaws might kill Josie without compunction once they had their hands on the necklace. They'd already killed twice. What was to stop them from just outright killing her? Especially if she started asking questions, which Taylor already knew she planned to do. He hadn't bothered to try to talk her out of it. Nothing stopped Josie or any of her sisters, for that matter, from doing what they wanted.

Adelaide had said that Josie was shy and didn't really take part in the investigations, other than office work. She certainly didn't seem shy or withdrawn to Taylor. She was vibrant and energetic, and adventurous. She was filled with courage and bravery. Either Adelaide and her sisters were wrong—which he doubted—or Josie had changed. Maybe she was in the process of changing, and he was helping facilitate that.

He was nervous and confident at the same time. If it had just been a simple case of extortion and all they wanted was the necklace to leave him alone, he would have gladly given it. But they'd already killed twice, and he didn't trust that they wouldn't do it again. Josie would ask questions, and they would be suspicious. If they gave her the answers she wanted, they would have to kill her. They would know she would report to the police as soon as she could.

Josie trying to get confessions would be her downfall. He couldn't wait till they were in there talking to her. He had to be in that room. He had to get in there and be with her when it went down.

Taylor turned and frantically looked around the compartment he was in. He didn't know how he would get Josie out of hers so he could get in, but he would find a way. His eyes roamed all around the room, looking for a place to hide. This compartment would be identical to hers, so if he found a place in here, he would find it in there.

He lifted his eyes and spotted the perfect place.

Now all he had to do was wait for her to leave her compartment. He hoped she would. There was no way he could lure her out. He racked his brain but couldn't think of anything, so he stood at the door, watching and waiting.

28

Josie was so very nervous. She stood just inside the door after talking to the deputy in the next compartment, kneading her hands together. Her throat was constricted, and her mouth was dry. She looked around the small room, feeling as if the walls were closing in around her.

After a few minutes, she turned around again and opened the door as quietly as she could. She looked to the left and the right but saw no one. She didn't even know if those men had gotten on the train. Maybe they were already in another city, waiting to board there instead.

She pressed her lips together, debating whether she should go to the dining car and get a drink. She was parched. Surely they had some tea or coffee. She didn't really want coffee, but if that's all they had to offer, that's what she would take.

She closed the door silently and hurried down the corridor toward the door that would let her into the next car.

Josie hesitated before opening the door that would let her into the next car. She was going to be tempted to look in each window for the men she was supposed to meet. She didn't want to annoy or alert them, though. She wanted them to have to come and find her.

She quickly decided to continue. She wouldn't let those men scare her so much. She would get herself a drink and just forget about them for a few minutes.

Lifting her shoulders, she went through the door and marched down the corridor, quietly but confidently. She made no noise and didn't turn her head to look in any of the compartments. There was a good chance her hat and fancy dress would give her enough of a disguise if they only saw her for a moment as she passed.

By the time Josie got to the dining car, she regretted having left her compartment at all. She asked for a hot tea. One was poured for her, and she took the cup, heading right back where she came from, not taking even one sip.

Back in her car, she walked softly to the door of her compartment and opened it, momentarily afraid the two men would already be there, waiting for her.

They weren't.

She breathed a sigh of relief and went to sit by the window to sip her tea.

She'd only managed a few sips when the open space of the door she'd left partially open was filled by a large man. She looked up and saw it was the dark-haired foreign fellow.

Her entire body tensed up, and the cup shook in the saucer she was gripping. She loudly set the cup down on a small table jutting out of the wall, and stood up.

"H-hello," she said. The necklace burned like a hot coal in her pocket. She didn't know what else to say.

The two men came in without greeting her. They were followed by a third, a man Josie immediately suspected was responsible for the break-in at the Jameson house.

He was also the only one carrying a gun, a small one hidden in his bulky hand. He was much larger than the other two and looked like he'd had a particularly rough life. His face was full of scars, and she saw tattoos on his neck and under the cuffs of his jacket.

She swallowed and tried to step back, but she was already against the bench seat and the wall.

"Where is the necklace?" the blond-haired man spoke as usual.

"I have it," Josie responded, gathering every ounce of courage she had in her body, "but I want to know why you want it. We are prepared to give you a good deal of money instead if you will take it. Still, we don't know how you even know about it. It's a family heirloom—"

"Not *your* family," the tall foreign man cried out angrily.

Josie cringed, her eyes snapping to his face and then to the gun in the hand of the big man behind him at an angle.

The blond lifted one hand abruptly, and the other man sulked.

"That's enough, Vincent," the blond snapped, never taking his eyes from Josie's face. He relaxed his features into a pleasant smile, and Josie knew how he'd gotten his way in other situations. "This item is a special artifact, a piece of jewelry that is not only worth a great deal of money but also has significant ties to a war that was carried out between our families."

Josie wanted to say her family wasn't involved in any of it, but she didn't want to push her luck. She let him continue, listening to the long drawl of the man's tone, his slow words said with distinction in a voice a teacher might use to teach something complicated to unintelligent students.

"Many years ago, a war was fought for this necklace, not just a war of wealth and power but one of love and passion. The necklace was a gift from our ancestor, the King of Nabimi, to Princess Lavinia to show his true devotion and love. She turned her back on him and betrayed him, denying him."

"Princess Lavinia was killed at a very young age," Josie couldn't help speaking up. "Surely, her family has paid enough of a price. How could you continue the killing all the way until now? The deaths of two innocent women... their blood is on your hands."

"Not mine," the man said calmly, lifting both his hands in the air as if to prove it to her. "If there is blood to be spilled, I am not the one who spills it. That would be Frankie. He is the one who enjoys the killing."

Irritation slid through Josie. She turned her eyes to the big man with the gun. "You killed Becky and

Clara because you like to kill people? They were completely innocent."

"Perhaps now I will kill you..." The man lifted his pistol and pointed it at her.

Josie sucked in a sharp breath. To her surprise, the blond reached up and grabbed the killer's arm.

"She has not revealed the whereabouts of the necklace. You may do with her what you will after we have it."

"That doesn't give me a good reason to tell you where it is, does it?" Josie demanded. The necklace was practically burning her. She could feel it. She wondered if it was really all in her mind or if the gem would burn through her fabric and fall to her feet on the floor.

"Oh, you will tell us," the blond said, stepping toward her, lifting one hand in the air. She cringed, blocking the blow with both hands.

The strike never came. Before he could hit her, an overhead compartment door popped open, and Josie watched with astonishment as Taylor leaped from it and tackled the blond, pulling his arm away from her. The two men tumbled to the side, and Josie screamed at the top of her lungs.

The dark-haired man went for the two struggling men, trying to get his hands on Taylor. The man with the gun came for Josie. She ducked and dodged him, hopping up on the bench seat and scooting around him to come up behind him.

She saw the door of her compartment fly open, and the deputy jumped in. He was on Vincent less than a second later, pulling him away from Taylor and the blond man who were still rolling on the floor, wrestling, and throwing punches.

Josie wanted to help Taylor, but she knew he didn't need it. The deputy certainly didn't need her help. And the man with the gun was now facing her, his face a fiery ball of fury.

She had to think quick.

29

The big man seemed to loom over her, and once again, Josie slipped past him, hopping over the men on the floor launching punches at each other. The deputy was dragging Vincent out the door into the hallway, where they too began to wrestle with each other in the small confined space of the corridor.

Josie could hear people coming out of their cabins, curious to see what was going on. She heard a woman cry out in fear.

The next moment, she felt fingers grasp at her bonnet, gathering all the hair on her head in with it. Unwilling to lose a clump of hair on top of her head, she moved with the man's hand as he pulled her close to him. He swiftly let go of her hair and wrapped his great hand around her neck from behind. He began to squeeze.

Her airway was immediately closed off. She fought against the panic, her eyes looking down at the gun in his hand. Thoughts raced through her mind. She had to get out of his grip. Her fingers clawing at his weren't doing any good.

Josie had to do something before she passed out. She looked down at Taylor, who was in a similar position except he was on his knees on the ground and the blond was behind him crawling back up from having been knocked down. He reached out for Taylor.

Taylor pulled one arm up in front of him and brought his elbow back so that it connected directly with the blond man's face. The blond was knocked back, and blood spurted from his nose and upper lip. Taylor spun around and leaped on top of him, spinning him around and yanking both his arms back, so he had control of the blond man's hands. Meanwhile, the blond was shrieking in anger.

Josie did her best to mimic what she'd just seen Taylor do. Her elbow didn't have to be strong to be a sharp tool that could be used for her benefit. Unfortunately, she had no idea where her elbow would hit and if it would make much of a difference.

She felt the impact of her sharp elbow some-where on the big man behind her and had no idea where it had hit. It was the right place, though. She heard the man grunt in pain, and suddenly his hand was gone.

She thought quickly, turning around and kicking out with all her strength, yanking her skirt up with both hands. Her boot connected with his groin, and he bent over, yelling out in pain.

Josie reached out and snatched the gun from his hands, turning it around and backing up slightly, pointing it at the man.

She looked at the blond on the ground strug-gling against Taylor's strong grip. Outside in the corridor, she saw the edge of both Vincent and the deputy where the lawman had the outlaw up against the train wall.

"That's enough," she yelled. "I have the gun. Don't move another muscle."

Taylor looked over at her, a look of pride on his face so intense it made Josie's heart bounce in her chest.

"Good job, Josie," he stated. "Really good job."

Josie grinned, just giving him a glance because she didn't want to take her eyes from the big man who had almost choked her to death. She placed one hand briefly on her neck and then put it back on the gun to hold it steady. This was no time to break down in a case of nerves.

The deputy, having secured Vincent's hands behind his back, came into the compartment and slowly took the gun from her hands. She let him take it and slumped back against the wall behind her. Taylor was off the blond man moments later when the deputy gave him a rope to tie the man up. He came directly to Josie and took her in his arms.

Josie had never felt more secure in her entire life. Her nerves were still jumping, her heart pounding, and she felt like she was on the verge of crying. She didn't know why. The danger was passed. But she still felt like bawling her eyes out.

"It's okay, Josie," Taylor murmured, holding her close, patting her hair with his hand, and kissing her head periodically. "It's all right. Everything is taken care of now. You did it. You solved my case. Congratulations, Josie. Your first solo case successfully solved with no harm done."

Josie was grateful for his comforting words. She wished she'd been there sooner to prevent the two women from losing their lives. But if they hadn't died, the case wouldn't have come to her in the first place.

She put her arms around Taylor, relaxing against him for a moment.

"I hate to say it," the deputy got their attention by speaking up, "but we're gonna have to wait with these fellas till we get to the next stop. Maybe you want to go in a different compartment. I'll wait in this one with them."

Taylor looked down at Josie. "There's an empty one a few down. I was in there before I came in here."

"How did you manage that anyway?" Josie asked curiously, moving her eyes to the small area he'd popped out of. "That looks way too small to fit a man your size."

"It's bigger than you think," Taylor replied, amusement in his tone. "I'll show you when we get to the other one."

Josie laughed softly as they left the cabin. "That won't be necessary. I'll take your word for it."

"Are you sure?" Taylor teased. "It's really quite interesting how you have to fold your body to fit into somewhere like that. I'll tell you, I'm not sure I would have lasted much longer in there."

Josie shook her head and rolled her eyes. They stepped into the empty cabin, and Taylor closed the door behind them, pulling the drape. He followed her when she went to sit on the bench near the window. She turned to face him, and he faced her, clasping their hands together in between them.

"Thank you for doing what you did and saving me, Taylor."

He shook his head. "No. I should be thanking you. You solved my dilemma. You saved my family and me. Those men were dangerous, and you put yourself in between them and me. More importantly, you put yourself between my children and them. That's the way I see it. You put an end to the danger and the fear and the terror. My children can live without fear."

Josie bit her lips together, blinking at him. "If that necklace was the object and the cause of a war between two nations, those three men in there aren't the end of it. You will have to make contact with your relatives overseas and find out just what happened. You've got to go to the source, go to whoever sent these men until you stop this. I fear they will keep coming after you."

She could see Taylor hadn't thought of that. He didn't look afraid, though. He looked contemplative and determined.

"You are right," he said. "I've got my work cut out

for me. There is one thing I want to do first, though before anything else."

Josie's heart jumped in her chest. "What's that?" she asked.

He looked her directly in the eye and said, "I want to check on Kenny. I have a bad feeling he didn't give my address to them willingly."

EPILOGUE

The woods around the cabin were overgrown. Vines crept up the side of the building, hiding the walls from view at many different angles. The windows were nearly black with thick dirt caked on the panes of glass.

Josie stepped carefully over the fallen twigs and branches, her footsteps causing crackling that echoed through the air around her. Taylor was in front of her. He'd already made it to the door and was looking back over his shoulder at her.

"Be careful on those steps," he said. "It looks like somebody took a hammer to them. A big hammer. Come up the left side, and you should be safe."

Josie did as she was told, holding her hand up to

him when she was close to the top. He took her hand and steadied her till she was beside him. She looked around, a feeling of despair filling her. There was a distinct odor in the air, an unpleasant one that she always associated with a dead animal. It wasn't far from believable that there would be a dead animal somewhere around here. There were likely several dead animals around.

Taylor and Josie had continued on the train to Oklahoma, where Kenny Dawson's last known address was, according to Julia. They had stopped at the postmaster's office and asked for a direct house and were sent to the cabin with the warning that Kenny didn't like visitors and they might be shot on sight. They'd also been told that it had been some time since anyone in town had seen Kenny.

Josie thought she knew why. The state of the cabin told her before they even went inside.

Once the door was open and they were inside, Josie knew what the smell was originating from. It wasn't a dead animal. Not really.

She turned around and went back out immediately, unwilling to see what she knew would be a gruesome sight.

Taylor stayed inside. She could hear him moving

around and talking to himself at one point. At least, she hoped he was talking to himself.

Josie crossed her arms over her chest and stuck her head in the open front door. "Taylor?"

"Yeah, he's in here," Taylor called from a room in the back. "Don't come back here. I think animals got to him."

"That's what I'm going to believe anyway," Josie murmured, turning away from the doorway and staring out over the overgrown front yard.

A few moments later, Taylor was beside her, putting his arm around her shoulder and turning her, so she was pulled into a hug. It surprised her, but she welcomed it.

"I'm sorry you lost your brother-in-law, too. What a horrible situation."

"You know what the worst thing about it is?" Taylor murmured. She could hear the pain in his voice. "The necklace wasn't part of Becky's or Kenny's family. It was part of *my* family. It's *my* family's heirloom. And they are the ones who paid the price for it."

"That's awful, Taylor," Josie responded, pulling away to look up into his eyes, "but you can't blame yourself. Don't do that to yourself. It's not right."

He shook his head. "I don't blame myself. But it's

hard not to think about it like that. It's the truth, after all."

She took hold of his upper arms in her hands and held on tightly. "I'm going to help you get to the bottom of this, Taylor. There's nothing that can be done but accept what's happened, right? You said that yourself. You have to move on. So now, it's time to complete the mission, so no one else will lose their lives because of this." She reached in her pocket and pulled the necklace out, dangling it in front of him. He looked at it and then at her.

"It will look beautiful on you," he whispered softly. "As beautiful as it ever as on Princess Lavinia."

"Are we going to have to go to the island where she lived to find the truth and stop the war that's still going on if it is?" She raised her eyebrows.

Taylor blinked at her, his face neutral. "We might. Is that something you would be interested in doing?"

"I won't mind a little adventure," she said, smiling at him. "I think I'm getting used to it. It's exciting. A lot more exciting than filing papers in a cabinet and doing books."

Taylor moved closer to her, plunging one hand under her bonnet and through the thick strands of her dark hair. His gaze in her eyes was so intense it flooded her body with tingles.

"You will have to marry me before then." His voice was filled with passion. Josie's body heated up until she felt like she was on fire.

"I will marry you before then," she replied breathlessly, "if that is what you wish."

"It is," he replied in a simple tone. "On a train."

She paused. "On a train?"

"Sure, why not?" He leaned close, his lips hovering over hers. "I will take you as my wife, and from that moment on, I will be your lion, your shelter, your strength. No one will ever hurt you as long as I am near."

She stood on her toes. "On a train, it is."

Tingles exploded through her body when he brought his lips to hers, kissing her with the passion of a massive bonfire with flames reaching into the sky. She felt like she was melting, slipping down to the floor when her knees buckled beneath her.

Taylor didn't let her drop. He reached around her waist with one long arm and hoisted her back up, holding her against him as he continued to kiss her. She grasped at him, clutching with her arms around his neck, returning the kiss until she was out of breath.

When they pulled apart, she did so reluctantly. From the fire she saw in his eyes, she knew he didn't want to let her go either.

"I am in love with you, Josie Salinger," Taylor said in a deep, ardent voice. "Now for the formal proposal.Will you be my wife?"

Josie nodded. "Yes. I will. I will marry you. I told you this. But now I say it formally." She bit back a giggle.

His gaze shifted from one of her eyes to the other. She hoped he could see her love for him the way she could see his.

"Let's get out of here," he said abruptly, taking her hand and pulling her down the left side of the steps where it was safer.

She went with him, ready to follow him to the ends of the earth—or the islands in question—and to have escapades with the man of her dreams.

"Slow down," she said with a laugh as he pulled her to the buggy.

He looked back at her. "I can't," he said. "I'm ready to start my new life with you. I want to get back to Sacramento and start sorting everything out. We have to decide where we're going to live. I need to decide what to do with my business if we go on a long trip around the world. There's so much to do and no time to waste."

Josie laughed, climbing up in the buggy. His excitement was catching. She couldn't wait to see what the future had in store for her and her adventurous man.

Click here for more Blythe Carver books!

Sign up for the newsletter to be notified of new releases.

Click on link for
Newsletter
or put this in your browser window:

landing.mailerlite.com/webforms/landing/p6l2s1

www.ingramcontent.com/pod-product-compliance
Lightning Source LLC
Chambersburg PA
CBHW020325160726
47992CB00004B/1696